Every Man Must Build a Home

L. A. Heberlein

Livingston Press
at
The University of West Alabama

ISBN 0-942979-91-5 library binding
ISBN 0-942979-92-3, trade paper

Library of Congress Catalog # 2001099095

Copyright © 2002 L. A. Heberlein

All rights reserved, including electronic text

printed on paper meeting or exceeding the
Library of Congress requirement for acidity content

Printed in the United States of America
Coth Binding: Heckman Bindery

This is a work of fiction.
Any resemblance to real characters is coincidental.

Typesetting: Joe Taylor
Cover Design: Amber Sullivan

Cover photo courtesy of HubbleTelescope
oposite.s+sci.edu/pubinfo
STSc1-PRC96-22a-May 9, 1996
Jeff Hester & Paul Scowen
(Arizona State University) & NASA

Proofreading: Heather Loper, Brett Young, Holly Martin,
S. C. Pendergrass, Zayne Smith, Renita Lampkin, Julian Tyler,
Russell Hill, Kerrie Harris, and Stephen Slimp

For Bill Ray and Ed Stein

Every Man Must Build a Home

If you believe in Nothing,
especially because you believe in Nothing,
you're forced to believe in the virtues of the heart
when you come across them.

André Malraux
Man's Fate

I'd been three days on a bad road. Rained on three times, sandblasted twice, dumped my bike one time, bad, asphalt to gravel to barbed wire. But the man didn't have to look at me that way. Nor did he have to set the beer down that way when he brought it.

I did have to drink it the way I drank it. It was wet. The second was cold. Third one tasted like beer. The sun was from straight overhead as I walked back out into it. I stood on the step and stretched my back.

If there were heat on me I would have already been stopped. Then there was no heat. Well, I always did say she had an even temper. The sky was hot, clear blue. I decided I was far enough from anywhere I didn't want to be. I had half a thousand dollars, a jacket pocket full of ground salamander eyes, plenty of matches, and all the time in the world.

So long after first light before any warmth. We were camped a few miles below Victor, Colorado, Swallow and I, in a valley Swallow spotted on a topo map, which we got to by slipping through a barbed-wire fence and following a deer trail for several hours. I didn't have the right equipment, slept in a cotton bag. Going down was fine, warm from the fire still. Sleeping in my coat, head down inside the bag, I was comfortable until dawn. Not after.

I don't know who said the darkest hour is just before the dawn, but I know it isn't true. The darkest hour of night—and I have sat up many a long, dark night, you may believe me when I speak to you—varies, with the time of the moon's rising and setting, the shiftings of cloud. It bears no correlation to the time of dawn. The simplest among us should not expect darkness to be so regular.

But there is a correlation between cold and the coming of light. The closer to light, the longer you've been without heat. The coldest hour is just after dawn. Illumination doesn't cut the still-increasing bitterness only stirs the dawn wind to drive it further through you.

It was light when the cold woke me. I lay in a shivering ball, knowing that when light comes warmth follows, knowing also I had never been so cold, knowing I was getting colder, cold cutting through me like highway wind through a radiator screen.

There is nothing like cold. When the cold is bitter enough it will drive you from even what little protection you have, out further into it. Anything is better than huddling while it kills you.

So I walked, hunched like the cold ones hunch, up and down the creek bed, hopping up and down, studying the place where that luscious yellow ball should be, whimpering love songs to myself, thinking of Swallow, warm asleep in his blue down bag, watching the patches of straight sunlight high on the hills, radiance up there but none in the valley, none for hours to come.

It was—it is—a long time. You should try it some time. You will think it is your entire lifetime, waiting there in the dawn wind. Perhaps you will be right. I don't know.

I do know that when warmth comes it is more than all the cold together. I saw a patch of yellow break over the striated monster of a mountain face before our camp, fall down at the valley's end, where the creek turns to find the lake. I sprinted down to meet it, twisting my ankle on a rock halfway. There is nothing like feeling the sun sink into your skin. I stood in it and loved it as I have never loved anything anywhere inside my life: immediate, powerful, true. I walked up with it as it slowly climbed the valley.

But then, of course, there is nothing like Swallow, for bringing you back. When he finally woke, around noon, he asked me how I had slept. I told him my story. He gave me that look of his, then he asked, in that voice of his

—Why didn't you just build a fire?

> *There is Nothing to be afraid of.*
> R.D.Laing
> *The Politics of Experience*

In May of 1974, when he was twenty-three, Alan Swallow decided to kill himself. I don't think there were any immediate reasons. The world can be empty and painful for a man of that age. His body was a pleasureless place, hard and cold as barbed wire, and, like coils of wire, tense with the energy of a spring, ready to snap and lash out, but not snapping, not lashing, just continuing to lie coiled tight and rusting. He did not appreciate anything about himself or his life. He actively disliked the woman he lived with. He hated himself for the way he was with her.

Her name was Joyce. She wore fuzzy things with cartoon pictures of animals on them. She liked French's mustard. She listened to Dionne Warwick. She watched television. Most of all, she liked who he pretended to be with her, and for that he could not forgive her. Or himself.

He sat in the claw-footed tub, letting it fill with bad-smelling water. They lived in the small mountain town of Nederland, Colorado, half an hour up the canyon west of Boulder, in a house her father had agreed to buy because when she finished school he could sell it and recoup all the expense of her four years.

It was hard to respect the house, which had been built as a mountain cabin. No insulation. Electric space heaters. The walls high varnished knotty pine, with scalloped window valances. Joyce had been there eight years, keeping up the payments. Swallow estimated that she paid each month more than the cost of materials in the original construction. Since she had bought it, the real estate value had tripled.

Nederland had an antiquated water system designed to supply a few summer cabins back in the thirties, before all these people moved in and started digging all these septic tanks. The water in the tub smelled like percolated shit.

He heard two dogs barking across the valley. One suddenly howled. There was a gunshot. The other dog went crazy, yelping.

The valley was tense. The young people from far places had taken over —culturally, politically, economically, physically. They had taken over the Pioneer. They had taken downtown, the hillsides, the roads and the streets.

The old people who had lived there before sometimes killed the young people's dogs. The young people sometimes killed the old people's dogs. At night the dogs would pack up, unconcerned about which group their owners belonged to. In February the dogs had killed a ten-year-old.

Everyone was buying guns. At the Pioneer Inn last Tuesday night a young man with red mustaches, from Iowa, wearing a three hundred dollar pair of blue climbing boots, had tried to sell Swallow a forty-five. There was talk of dynamite.

As the tub filled, Swallow looked at his forearms. He had spent years staring at them, tripping, as they turned red, white, and purple, coiling, limp somehow, like wet paper, sad, the little hairs in them, the tissue too bloodless or too blood-filled. Life as protoplasm looks like this, Swallow thought, no matter how pornographers try to soften the focus.

He held a straight razor with a mother-of-pearl handle. The razor was his grandfather's. His grandfather had taken to using safety razors when Swallow was in junior high. About the time they built all the houses. Swallow looked at the arteries near his wrist. He knew to slit lengthwise. He had chosen a pleasant and effective method. Girls could eat pills and wait around to be discovered. He wanted to kill himself.

He shut off the water and closed his eyes. He tried to summon up an image. His sensibility demanded that he have a clear picture in his mind as he went out. Something to encapsulate it. Something bitter and rasping and utterly clear.

He couldn't find it.

—You are looking for your true love.

Swallow, ten years old, dressed in blue jeans, t-shirt, and sneakers, accompanied by his dog, a terrier-collie mongrel who had come, like all dogs, from the highway one afternoon, was down in the pasture. He was on his knees in the thin red dirt, on the side of a rounded bump of fill dirt covered with chokecherry bushes, at the very bottom of the pasture, in the hollow where the water ran in spring. It was August. There was no water. The thistles and quackgrass were yellow. Swallow was digging a hole. He came down each day after lunch and dug with an army-surplus camp shovel, handle only two feet long, which he had found abandoned in a ditch. Each evening before he returned to the house for supper he covered the hole with old one-by-tens. He was not searching for buried treasure, nor did he seek the other side of the planet. He wanted to build an elaborate underground empire in which he could rule alone. He wanted it invisible in the pasture bottom, a dirt-covered hole in the bramble of chokecherry bushes the only entrance, and underneath it his laboratories, machines, and library.

Swallow had not seen the magician approach. He had been digging absent-mindedly, staring into the hole but thinking about birds, and he was startled by the stranger's voice.

—You are looking for your true love.

The stranger was tall. His beard, nearly to his waist, was gray—not the woolen gray of his long robes, but a silver gray like clouds after sunset. Though his robe had no stars, though he carried no book, Swallow knew he was a magician.

—Listen carefully to me, the magician said. You will not see me again for many years, and I have much to tell you. You are looking for your true love.

—But I'm not.

—You are looking for your true love, though you do not know it yet. You'll not find her now. You'll not find her until you have grown old and grown young again. Before you find her you will walk through fire. You'll not find her until you have been king of all that lives and much that dies, been a good king and a bad king and then no king, been a broken, friendless beggar, blind, despised and despairing. Every breath you take you take for her. Your eyes are for her. Your mouth is for her. Your heart is for her. Your legs and your arms and your mind-to-be are for her. You will spend them looking for her and not find her till you've spent them. On your way to her you will lie, kill, suffer countless hurts, and cause much pain to those you would heal.

A cloud covered the sun and the boy felt the sweat chill on his skin. Swallow listened to the magician as he listened to the priest at the temple, massaged by the melody, missing the meaning, though he listened to it hard, though he knew it was true, true in another sphere if not true for him now.

—Will I find her?

—You will find her. Not for many ages. On the way to her you will be mistaken six times. Six times you will fall in love with one who is not her, each time forgetting all you know and losing all you do not have. Six times you will give your soul up to her fair sisters. You will find her.

It was over, as the prayers at temple were in time over, so you could release the unnatural attention and sit naturally once again. Swallow looked down at his hole, knowing somehow that his underground empire was never to be again, that his shovel would rust in the pasture bottom. He stared a last time at the cool, firm earth below the hot, loose earth. When he looked up, the magician was six rods away, walking neither especially fast nor especially slow, toward the Duykink road.

Swallow then heard, though it had been ringing for he did not know how long, the supper bell. It was an unmusical flat-toned cowbell his mother had hung on the back porch to call her son in to supper. It was nowhere near suppertime. The bell rang frantically, hysterically. Swallow dropped his shovel, forgot to cover the hole with the one-by-tens, and ran as fast as he could up the long hill towards the house.

> *There is Nothing truer than myth.*
> Eugene Ionesco
> 'Experience of the Theatre'

He tried replaying painful things other kids had done to him when he was little. He thought about every one of his aunts, about teachers, about Agnew and Hitler and the war in Vietnam, still grinding on, the machinery of killing continuing to kill though no one believed any more it was for any purpose, they simply could not find a way to stop it. He thought about Kissinger overthrowing the democratically elected government of Chile. He thought about the scalloping over the kitchen sink.

He grew bored, restless, weary, as in those fights with Joyce when he'd keep working the conversation around until she'd be forced to say the one line so clotted with stupidity and malice that no one in the world could possibly misunderstand it if he recounted it later, so there could be no indecisive recrimination in his heart when he played back the scene, so he would know with absolute certainty that he was justified in leaving. And she'd always muff it, blunt it, say something silly rather than summative.

He thought how cold it was to put people on this planet and expect them to live here and then just have to die, and he thought about the mockeries of religion and philosophy, and he thought about the incredible crudity of history. None of it worked. Eventually he threw the razor across the room and watched it stick in the varnished pine.

When Joyce came home—the library closed at nine, then she had to give her friend Devin a ride, then come up the canyon—he had an even lamer fight with her than usual, told her he had to go into town, and took her car keys with him.

In the produce department of King Soopers, between cucumbers and mushrooms, he ran into T.J., his buddy since the second year of art school. T.J. said he was leaving in the morning for Richmond, Virginia, where he was returning Linda, Linda he'd lived with for three years, because she wanted not to live with him any more and wanted to go back to Richmond, with her dogs and clothes.

—Meet me there. We'll drive up to New York. I have a comic strip I'm trying to sell to the syndicate. We can stay at Lang's place in the Village. Then see my friend Freda in Boston and drive back. It'll be a good trip. I need another driver. It'll give us a chance to talk.

Why is it whenever you're utterly aimless, someone shows up with a plan? They agreed to meet in Richmond in a week.

When Swallow visits his kingdom, the people come running out to see him. They stand by the side of the dusty road, waving dishtowels as he rides by.

They give him time to settle in, unpack, and bathe, then, one by one, they come to the courtyard and wait patiently in line all day to tell him their needs.

The battlements are falling down. The irrigation system to the east valley needs patching, really needs rebuilding. Fighting, almost war, breaks out between the valley people and the hill people. Scouting parties for invaders have been regularly seen. The defense forces are in disarray. The markets have collapsed. The livestock are sick. Swallow's staff is charged with sloth and corruption.

He takes these issues to heart. When he rode for this land, he thought of all the things he would do here, construction projects, adventures, exploration, expansion. Hunts and revels. Now, it seems, his time here is to be all taken up with repairs.

Before he can even get work parties started, a messenger comes from the city with an urgent summons. He rides hard for the city, arrives without sleep on a worn horse, and then it is weeks of negotiate and parry, deal and deliver, stand up and talk. By the second week, he has forgotten his kingdom completely. He rises, works through a whole day, walks through the evening, falls into sleep, without his people ever once entering his thoughts. His people must feel this, in their valley, on their hills. They must know their king, in the city, does not think of them.

> *We see Nothing, then suddenly the name appears in its exact form and very different from what we thought we could make out.*
> Marcel Proust
> *In Search of Lost Time*

Swallow decided to take the train, hoping to meet people. See some scenery. Feel the rocking of the rails. He was twenty-three years old and had never been on a train. He had never been east of Kansas. What better than to see America for the first time from his first train?

The train was three hours late arriving at Union Station. There were seat reservations nowadays, now that it was Amtrak, only it seemed everyone on the train had been given the same reserved seat. No dining car, it had caught fire in Glenwood Canyon. No air conditioning, either. He found a corner of the club car and watched people drink. In the morning he realized he had slept, realized he hurt, and realized that the train was full of androids.

Well, first he realized that the young soldier with the black hair was an android. The way his skin was knit on the back of his neck. Human skin was seamless on the back of the neck, but androids had seams, as it stands to reason they would.

Swallow earnestly examined other necks. With the women you couldn't tell.

Was there another way to tell? Watch the soldier. Do his elbows work perfectly? His elbows seemed to work perfectly. Swallow talked with him. His speech was okay. There weren't any pronunciation problems, there wasn't anything in the sentence contours.

That's it. There wasn't anything. Every contour was a contour Swallow had heard before. They were programmatic. Of course they were programmatic. They were programmed.

Who else talked like that?

Joyce talked like that. He had never heard her say anything he had never heard before. Okay. Joyce was an android. That explained a lot.

Who else on the train was an android? What were they doing there? Who was introducing androids into the human population? And how many of them? By the time they pulled into Chicago he decided it was about half the train.

There was a three-hour layover in Chicago. He walked down to the lake, ogling the city, wondering if he had time to try a ride on those elevated trains. Every city should have those. So you could ride above the city, looking down on it. The breeze as he walked was bracing. When he got to the lake, he found a microscopic patch of grass before a Coast Guard station, lay down and thought it through. Forget *Invasion of the Body Snatchers*. Someone local is going to the trouble of building these things. But why?

Why anything? There's only ever one answer. Because money.

But that didn't make sense. Protoplasm is free. These things must be expensive to manufacture.

But only to manufacture. After that, you could be sure they wouldn't try to overthrow the government. You could count on them as soldiers.

Were they introduced randomly, or were they seeded? Were particularly troublesome individuals replaced at night? He thought back over his acquaintance. How about Pharaoh Feldman? One day Pharaoh had that hair all the way out to his shoulders, and the next time Swallow saw him he was working in a bank and you couldn't talk to him at all, it was like there was a layer of language he'd just suddenly stopped understanding.

Swallow walked slowly back uptown, stopping frequently to stare at people. He got back on the train and saw the soldier exchanging glances with the porter.

If you can't trust your own subjective impression of reality, what can you trust?

Swallow knew they were going to kill him, and it was suddenly very important to him to be alive. He stepped off the train and walked quickly through the station.

When he got outside he realized his bag was on the train. The Amtrak people wouldn't give him any money for his ticket. He had twenty dollars in his pocket.

Who did he know in Chicago?

Hell, he had a wife in Chicago.

He had spent forever, since way back before nothing, incorporating the materials of the mundane universe into the vast other universe which he believed, as one of the two acts of faith he allowed himself, was true.

After a heartless stretch of not ever seeing anything to convince him there was distance out beyond the low-budget set he played on, he all at once and without even noticing found the set transparent, so he could look through any piece of it. Any piece, a can of green beans on a grocer's shelf, look through it like looking through a leaded glass picture composed of infinitely many infinitely small refracting colored prisms, look not only through but into, find all *other* in it, and also see the things and nothings beyond and through it.

When he did this, he found he had no need to invent a new cognitive structure in which to think of the things he saw. He could simply use the structure provided by the set. If he were thinking of what he saw in the green beans, all he needed to remember was *green beans*. He could get there by going down past corn, artichoke hearts and peas. In this way, when he was thinking of things to himself, he was not stopped up by a lack of vocabulary. He could say, for instance, 'A green bean is seven steps further ostrich than terra cotta.'

Living in the whole space he could see, and thinking in it, exulting in his discovery, and in the ease of it all, in his innocent joy of discovery, he thought of one consideration, then plunged into the true terror of loneliness. Struggling frantically to get back inside after so long fighting to break through and free, he was dismayed to find, after eons fighting to see not just the set, that he was now locked as firmly outside it, in the prismatic beyond, where, glitter wearing off the edges of night, he began to notice they were no sweet-honey visions out there, but vast, sweeping motions, hideous and menacing attacks, not even impersonal but looking straight down the pipe at his quivering soul with venomous disgust. And once a man sees it, he can never not see it again, he could not come back inside, and they glared down at him like you glare at a bug in your oatmeal, he was alone in the awesome night with them, head full of stained-glass backwards and upside down, visions of a great, too-great beyond, and a hunger, and nowhere to go, alone, alone among his own kind, for he had lost their language, forgotten how to use it, as they did who saw only the set. He could not even call for help. He could never stop seeing, nor once more ever speak in human tongue.

> *If Nothing counteracts the natural consequence of learning, we grow more happy as our minds take a wider range.*
> Samuel Johnson
> *Rasselas*

It was her voice that answered, on the first ring.

—Hello?

—Hi kid.

A pause which sort of hurt his feelings, then —Tuko! Hey, babe, it's Tuke!

In the distance —Where's he calling from?

—How are you, Tuke? *Where* are you?

—In Chicago.

—What are you doing here? He's *here*, Jack.

—Ask him if he's had dinner.

—Tuke, come on over. We're just about to eat. It's just a snack, we both just got home this minute.

—I know about your snacks. I'd love to. Where do you live?

She volunteered to come get him. Swallow said he could get there on his own, and gave a cabby most of the twenty for a long ride out to a two-story white wooden house on a two-acre lot.

Swallow was in a housewares and gift shop, looking for a Valentine's Day present for Cindy. It was the first time he had been in such a store in years, maybe since that time he had thrown such a fit about Cindy's making him stand around watching her shop all afternoon.

It was Valentine's Day. Cindy, he knew, Cindy who cruised shops with friends for fun, Cindy to whom shopping was like listening to music, Cindy would have found the perfect present for him months ago. 'Oh, wouldn't this be perfect for Tuko,' she would say to Mary or whoever was with her. And it would be. It would be perfect. When he opened it, it would be something he never would have thought of ever buying for himself, but something he would use and appreciate and think of Cindy every time he did. Something off the beaten track, something you'd never see advertised.

Whatever he found for Cindy, she'd say, 'Thank you, dear. That's lovely.' And she'd give him a kiss and a hug. And then maybe she'd wear it once on a picnic with him, and then he'd never see that thing again. When she wore it to the picnic he would see why. It would be slightly the wrong size, or the wrong shade, or just not her at all.

Hell, Cindy sent back three-quarters of the things she bought for herself, and the fourth thing she repainted or ripped out the seams and re-sewed. If Cindy, the world's most precise and experienced shopper, couldn't find what she liked in the shops, what chance did he have, who only entered a shop two or three times a year when these occasions demanded? Who had no idea what was old hat and what was in the air?

It would even the decks, he thought, if instead of requiring a present on these days they required you to write a poem to your lover in a language you learned just for the occasion.

Beauty is Nothing by itself.
Immanuel Kant

Cin had lost ten or twenty pounds. She still had the rash on her chin. He heard the cough in her voice.

Jack came out of the den, offered his hand. —Swallow, old man, it's good to see you. What are you doing in our neighborhood? Can I offer you a drink?

Swallow saw one of his rice-paper paintings on the den wall. —You, too. Passing through. Sure, I'd love one.

He tried not to stare. The last time they'd met, Jack had been a longhaired Chicano smack freak in a four-by-seven room over a TV repair shop on the North Side of Denver. Swallow had been there to take some books back to Cin. *Antigone* and Nathalie Sarrautte. He'd found a scab-ridden, skinny body on her kitchen table. Not quite at ease, she'd said—That's Jack.

Was Jack an android now? Or was it just what Cindy did for a man? Jack was six foot, two hundred solid pounds, in burnt-walnut pants and a Mexican wedding shirt, his hair hot-combed.

—You're looking good, Jack.

—I have to put in an hour of tennis every morning to keep from going to blubber. Let me remember, you're a Scotch drinker?

—Bourbon. Turk if you got it.

How could he sneak a peek at Jack's neck? Or did it matter? Cin went back into the kitchen. He'd wanted to look a while longer at the sweater she'd been wearing. He couldn't figure out how it was done.

— This is a beautiful house, Jack.

It was a beautiful house. It was not just the verticality of it, though Swallow, coming from the west where everything was 'ranch' style one-story, balloon-framed houses, did find lovely melodies in the house's use of the third dimension, in the tall entryway, in the sweep of the staircase down the middle of the house. It was more the materials. Everywhere you looked was wood the way wood was worked a hundred years ago. Big hunks of high-grade materials you couldn't get today no matter how much you were willing to pay, and shaped for hours by old woodworkers whose kind had died out at least two generations back. Box beams across the dining room with joints and moldings Swallow would have liked time and privacy to record it all in a sketchbook. Yet here he was in the suburbs. The wood didn't work here. Or needed redefinition. Where Swallow came from, houses in suburbs were two or three years old, not a hundred, built fast by sub-minimum-wage pick-up crews hired by out-of-state corporations, using skinny struts that hadn't even dried yet, floors bowing and walls cracking, the driveway just a painted concrete line in front. But this idea of a suburban culture that predated the automobile, back before everything became shoddy, meant he would have to rethink that word.

Jack waved one hand to pantomime dismissal and a comradely near-exasperation. —I never get a chance to live in it. You know how it goes. Money or time, pick one. Sometimes we get ten minutes after dinner to sit in the front room, put our feet up and have a dish of ice cream. Monday's my day off, I sleep all day.

—You got a restaurant here, is that what Cin wrote?

—Four. Just opened the fourth. I don't know why. I got to go down to that one right now. New manager, new staff. I don't know what they use for imagination. You'd think they were androids. If you're standing right there to tell them, they can figure it out, but if you aren't there and it's a fork instead of a spoon they can't make the leap.

Jack and Cin kissed at the kitchen door, Cin giving him that extra hug Swallow knew, the warm, small palm sliding down his back.

What was that crack about androids? Was that teasing? Hell, in two and a half years he hadn't found a situation that could bring a glass of alcohol to his lips, and here he was embarrassed not to drink in front of his wife's husband. Ex-wife. You're supposed to say 'the ex.' Not 'my wife.' You walk forward one day at a time, and one day when you're eight hundred days away from your last drink you're suddenly only one. Did it matter? There was only ever the same one day, anyway.

It would be reasonable to want to know who I am, and how I know these things. I knew Swallow years later, when he became the second husband of my ex-wife. We would see each other in passing, on Saturdays, when I was picking my son up at their house, or at school functions, or, it being a small town, in the grocery or at a play. He always seemed a reasonable sort of person, with a nicely understated wit and a calm unflappability, and it seemed obvious to the both of us that were it not for Theresa between us, we would immediately sit down to be friends.

When Theresa died three years later—well, not to put too fine a point on it, when Theresa killed herself one bright blue October morning, when Theresa made as big and splattered a mess of herself as she could possibly manage—Swallow and I spent a great deal of time together cleaning up and being solid for Jamie. We shared everything we could with each other and, that spring, it being ridiculous to maintain two households, we moved in together and Jamie no longer had to go back and forth each week.

So Jamie had, as they say, two fathers. And though both Swallow and I continued to go out with women, and occasionally spend a night away, neither of us was motivated to make another permanent attachment after Theresa, so it was the three of us there, in that drafty farmhouse. With a big enough fire in the Franklin, enough spaghetti boiling to steam up the windows, and maybe a friend or two of Swallow's dropping by with a mandolin or a fiddle, it felt like a home you wanted to come home to. Jamie's friends found it a sympathetic place to hang out, and it became a bit of a 'house of guys,' a place you could swear, fart, and put your feet on the coffee table.

Jamie is leaving for university in the fall, and that will be strange. I can no longer imagine life without Swallow. But this big bag of a house is too much for two old men. We have talked cabins on freighters around the Cape of Good Hope, small villages in the Sonoran desert. That may be

Swallow, but it is certainly not me. I have some interest in rebuilding an old warehouse downtown into condominiums. It's a beautiful brick building from the late nineteenth century. I can imagine it as a buzzing hive for singles young and old, a few families, the odd duck like me. An assemblage, like a house party. I have never built anything, and I think it is time to try. Swallow shakes his head and brings up one intimidating practical detail after another, but I can see that (like a man who resists adopting a cat), it is only because he is soft for the idea himself, and I feel I shall soon wear down his feigned resistance.

Nothing can make water better.
—Ursula K. Le Guin

Cin made dinner. It was as he remembered. She was surprised when he offered to help clean up after. She declined the offer, laughing and shaking her head.

— So you just rattle around this place all day?

—I didn't write you about the shop? I guess it hasn't been that long.

— Like you used to talk about?

— Jack finally got enough ahead so he could set me up. It's just a little storefront.

— You sell your hangings.

—Well, the consignment stuff pays the rent, but I've got a weaving class on Tuesday nights, I teach the little girls and grandmothers, and Tuke, I've got my own *wheel* in the back, and Jack is helping me synthesize *glazes*. . .

— You pot?

She looked at him as one looks at a stranger. —You . . . no, I guess you don't. Sometimes I spend all night there, the wheel and the . . . you didn't even notice the *dishes* you ate off?

He saw them drying in the rack.

—You wouldn't believe plates. Cups you can learn in about ten minutes, but *plates*, you have to work them up, just a skin of clay like the skin you peel off after you burn. Tuke, I'm starting to smith metals. Jewelry is so peaceful.

She caught a glimpse of the clock over the refrigerator—he realized the face was pottery and the hands cast—and dipped her white knuckles back into the suds. —And you? How is your painting going?

—I gave it up.

The coffee cup was not dropped but whisked, not before, but as she twisted, her hands already drying on the towel, to face him. —*Tuke*.

—Oh, you know, kid.

—Tuko, your *painting?*

The days she had counseled addicts, then dropped by the letter service on the way home, and weekends at the legal-ad newspaper, the days he sat in the porch he used for a studio, smoking endless cigarettes, keeping the butts and ashes in tin cans and taking them out to the alley before she got home, staring out the window at the neighbors' marigolds and at the squirrels, then at the progressively more meaningless geometric decompositions, and her asking, just before she fell into bed, how it went that day.

—Oh *Tuke*. She threw the towel down on the floor. —Tuke, your *painting*.

She picked up the towel and turned back to the sink, took his coffee cup and saucer—with elliptical leaves and broken twigs in a deep red—washed them out, then sat down at the table across from him, sat on her folded legs, the way she had always sat. She asked him about his sister and brother, his parents, his grandfather, a few uncles and aunts, T.J., friends in Denver. Then one more glance at the clock.

— I'm really sorry. I don't mean to be, I mean, I have a girl to come in and keep the shop over dinner, but I can't afford yet, I mean . . .

—That's cool. I should be going anyway.

—I wish you'd told us you were coming.

—Yeah, I know.

—Oh, listen, I found a book of your sketches, from when we were living on South Logan Street.

She went upstairs and returned with an envelope.

She looked at the clock again. —Hey, babe, listen, if you'd like to stay the night . . .

—No, I should go.

—We've got this whole place here, you can have your pick of rooms, tomorrow's Jack's slow day, and I can get Karen to . . .

—I really appreciate it, but I got a ride waiting for me.

—Then you'll have to come back. Are you coming back through this way? What are you doing, anyway, where you headed? You still live in Boulder?

—Up near Rollinsville.

—Oh, it must be beautiful this time of year.

—Yeah, I suppose.

—Listen, I really do have to rush. Karen will kill me. Listen, you really should come by. You know you're welcome.

—Yeah.

—I mean really. Jack asks me every once in awhile why I don't get you out here.

Then another glance at the clock, a dart into the other room, returning with a hand-cut bag, crickets in lively colors. Two thick ledgers. A set of keys.

—We can't talk you into staying? We'll go to the park tomorrow. I'll make a picnic.

—I'm really due elsewhere.

She drove him in a gold Volvo station wagon, with fusion jazz on the tape deck. She dropped him at the transit stop he said to drop him at.

—Well it's wonderful to see you, Tuke. It would be good to see you more. Come back when you can stay.

—I will.

—Okay.

She started to drive off, then stopped, reversed, rolled down the passenger side window.

—Tuke, I'm sorry, I didn't even ask. I mean, do you need any money?

His denial was quick, absolute, stammeringly earnest. She leaned all the way across the seat out the window to look at his eyes.

—I don't want you to put me off, now. Do you need any money?

—Honest. I'm fixed okay.

—All right. You take care of yourself.

—I will.

Swallow waited until she had turned a corner, then started hitching. It took three rides to get out of town, then he had to wait several hours, until after midnight, before he could get a cross-country lift. Two teachers headed to a summer seminar at Vanderbilt.

In the morning, while the tall one, the brunette, was in the motel shower, he took out the book of sketches. They were worse than he remembered.

You go through the smoky valley and find a clean plateau. You go through the tortuous tunnel and step out onto the infinite open. You go through the whitest water and come to the cleanest pool.

Gliders hang by nothing high above a lesser place. There is stillness, and the sound of motion. You look at them from the ground, think them frivolous, want to be there.

From the valley it looked like a big black hole in the overhanging mountain, out of which strange creatures sometimes crept. Some of the few who went exploring in it told stories of gleaming crystal caverns, others tales of side exits onto gardens, deserts warmed by alien suns. Many who went in did not come back. I lived in that place then. When I wandered back out into Swallow's valley, it was as if the valley were only another of the caverns.

Swallow slept his one black hour, got up and went into the real world. The real world released him at noon. He ate lunch at Vee's Kitchen and then went to Uncle Sugar's General Store on East Colfax. Armed guards surveyed him at the door. Uncle Sugar's was crowded. Every time Swallow worked up the strength to enter the store he found it more crowded than the time before. The aisles were clogged with human flesh, rancid, wet, irritable. Fat housewives scolded and slapped loud children; secretaries with long, sheathed legs looked disdainful; tribes of muddy, patched, easily-laughing athletic males in sweaty t-shirts told cheap stories; store clerks were busy hating being there, hating the endless murmur of noise, the crush of annoyances, the imprisonment. Swallow skirted the crowd and looked for a clear aisle to the back of the store. He hated 'excuse me' encounters, and would walk three aisles out of his way to avoid one. All the narrow aisles were jammed as far back as he could see. Resignedly he edged his way into one and 'excuse-me'd' his way past two uniformly brown, flat-chested young girls with gold-brown hair picking over sheer black bikini panties while eating gumdrops (they did not look up); a bald middle-aged man in a red golf shirt and blue-flowered Bermuda shorts pushing a metal basket full of boxes and bags mostly full of air adorned with bright colorful trademarks (he gave Swallow a wide yellow smile of brotherhood; Swallow did not meet his eyes); a thin, aged . . . but there were many of them, thirty, maybe, before he made it to the back of the store.

At the back of the store was a dairy case, open-faced, filled with cardboard cartons of milk. Swallow approached them as a skittish stallion approaches a barbed wire fence then stared, stared at the two-color print on the waxed paper cartons, as if enough looking, or the right kind of looking, would let his eyes unfocus, no longer see the printed brand names but instead some huge emptiness beyond them. As if holding to some last kernel of faith that beyond the milk cartons was the emptiness, and beyond the emptiness a final trilling rose of fire.

The law gives us Nothing
William Carlos Williams
'Desert Music'

The ride out of Nashville left him somewhere in the Tennessee hills he felt he'd rather not be, and warned him about hitching further. He was standing on the sidewalk for about thirty seconds when the local constabulary asked him what he was doing.

—I was just going into this bar here.

—You passing through? Where's your car?

—My friend went off to get gas and some groceries. I was just going in to have a drink.

—I don't know if Leroy wants longhaired Yankees that smell like they could have come off some commune drinking in his establishment.

—I'll just have a drink and wait for my friend and then we'll be off down the road.

—If we see you again, boy, we just might have to run you uptown and show you our new proctoscope, you hear?

After a few feet you begin to see through your companions, see their aching blue veins, the pools of their black phlegm, metal grid of their tensions, substanceless, you see the prismatic stalactites behind them, through them. Later they will tell you what they saw through you—sometimes. Other times you do not talk of it at all. Usually you talk in oblique inferences. It seems more appropriate, possibly more human.

Swallow's Aunt Millie married, as her second husband after his Uncle John died, a man whose brother was Howard Hughes' barber.

—*He come into the shop in '48,* said Aunt Millie repeating this man's words, *and asked for a haircut. I give him one. 'Why, you're . . .' I was about to say, but I knew he was on the lam from the Congress, it was in all the papers, so I didn't say nothing. I give him the haircut and I clam up when I can tell he don't want to hear no jokes, and hand him the mirror and said 'How you like her, Mr. . . . I mean sir,' and he smiles and he says, 'I like it just fine, Shorty. How'd you like to be my regular barber?' I say 'Sure!'*

—And then, don't you know, Aunt Millie continued, shaking the plastic pop beads around neck, the next week what arrives in the mailbox but a check for five hundred dollars, and a contract. And what do you suppose it says? It says he's to 'forego all other employment' and 'be ready to present his services when requested.' He signs the contract of course, don't you know, and mails it to the post office box in California, and takes himself home to wait.

—And then, she said, pushing her swoopy glasses up her nose, he waits, and he waits, and every month the check comes. That was twenty years ago, and the checks are still coming. He gives haircuts to his neighbors to stay in practice. He cuts Jim's here—Jim, honey, come here and show Margie and Mary your haircut.

> *Poetry makes Nothing happen.*
> W.H. Auden
> 'Yeats'

Swallow sat in the bar nursing a 7-Up. He hated 7-Up, hated the sugary taste. Swallow sat there hating the way it made his mouth all sticky and trying to think up some way out of where he was. This was one of those places where you could do lots of things. There are always lots of ways out of where you are.

When Swallow was a boy, the times he liked best with his father were driving into town after dinner in the '48 Ford, gray wearing off to show shiny plum primer beneath. His dad was a deacon at the church. Later he was an elder, and involved in ugly church politics, mostly about the new preacher's wife, but Swallow remembered when he was a deacon. The deacons visited old people who couldn't get to church, took meals to them and read the Bible. What Swallow remembered best was driving in to town at night to help out people who were passing through and had problems, their car broke down, or they got robbed, or once a man just dumped his wife as if she were a dog you'd drive out into the country with.

His dad would take them to Abe's Cafe and they'd all eat dinner, and then he'd find them a place to sleep, and then he'd give them an envelope of cash.

—Now don't try to return this before you should. The next fifty dollars you get, you spend it on food for that little girl there. Don't let her get hungry on account of your pride, now. You wait till you're back on your feet first.

They always sent the fifty bucks back. And his father would tell Swallow —Bad times can happen to anyone, Al. One little twist of luck is all it takes. And people look right through you as if you weren't even human any more.

His father would tell him —You ever get in trouble, Al, you go to the church. You'll find a phone number there on the side door, just like this one. You call it. You tell them you're a member of a congregation in Littleton, Colorado, you tell them what happened to you.

Swallow's eyes got a little misty as he thought about this now, but he did not try to find the church.

He thought about stealing a car. He had been an outlaw for a long time. Policemen had shot at him. He had spent time in jail. But he had never, like, *stolen* anything before. It seemed out of kilter to start now. He wondered if he could figure out how to hot-wire a car. Hell, it always said in the insurance blurbs that most cars had keys left right in them. This was a small town, there were probably six cars on Main Street he could just drive off in.

He did not steal a car. He couldn't imagine having the nerve to open the door of someone else's car. What if that somebody else happened to come out of the store just then?

There's probably a poker game going somewhere. He could parlay the three bucks he had left into a fortune. He did not do that either.

He could call Joyce and ask her to wire him money. He could call his parents. He could ask Leroy for a job washing dishes, sweeping up the back. He could stand in the shadows outside and try to jump on a truck. He could walk to the train tracks—there must be train tracks—and try to hop a freight. He had always wanted to do that.

He did not do any of these things.

What he did was what he always did. Swallow's approach to a serious problem was to try to find a woman to get him through it. He did not understand why other men did not do this. When women had problems, they were good at standing forlornly over the problem, advertising for help. When men had problems, they hid the problems under their jackets. Swallow had met a lot of nice women by requesting assistance.

Guys seemed to keep score of their lives by how many women they could sleep with, and they joked about how well Swallow always scored, some of them mean in their envy. But Swallow wasn't playing the same game, he didn't think. He was only trying to get warm, only trying to find the nearest laundromat. Sure, if they offered to let him use their washer, that would be nicer. Sure, he loved the way women softened when they softened. But it was somehow different than at least the way the other guys talked.

There was a woman in the bar. She was old, and she was drunk. She was wearing a white miniskirt and white boots. Her hair was bleached blonde and she wore makeup thicker than Iowa topsoil. He went over to her and sat down beside her. — I need help, he said.

He stayed with her two days and then agreed to take money from her for a bus ticket. He fixed up things in her house that she said had needed fixing ever since her late husband, Ray, died of a heart attack four years ago. Her house was sad, plaster falling off the laths. It was not so much house as shack. Swallow's Aunt Leona's chicken shack had thicker walls. He couldn't do anything about the walls, but he could see to simple wiring problems, so she could have light at least. She was really an interesting person, had a sharp wit and a reservoir of stories she didn't get chance enough to tell. He felt their exchange came out about even. It really works out, he thought. Each half can't make it. Bump them together even for two nights, and they both come away with more than they had before. He came away with a bus ticket.

Dear Swallow,

1. The Frisbee is on the front lawn.

2. Either two rent checks are attached to this note and you get to make up the third OR no rent checks are attached and you get to make up a good story when Sally comes by.

3. ALERT! This house is running dangerously low on cognac.

4. If you're missing anything, it's because I took it, I will either return it or you can bill me for it at monthly reconciliation, by when we ought to be back. If you're not missing anything, it's because I couldn't find it.

5. My plants have been dying for seven-odd years now, if they finally buy the big rose garden in the sky I'll let you have the pots for free. An expert I once met under truly bizarre circumstances which I will spare you in the interests of time told me they need to have water put on them once in a while.

6. If you find a job, would you get me one too?

7. If my mother calls, I am in Texas.

8. If Toni Brown calls would you give her my love sweet and slow six or seven times and tell her I have her jacket.

9. If any other female calls, please let me make my own mistakes, please take her number and I'll talk to her myself, please. Except if she's selling drugs, you can say we'll take all she's got, if she's offering credit.

10. If none of the above applies, I am sleeping under a heavy load, would you please cook an unbelievably big breakfast and wake me very gently.

L.A.Heberlein

> *Nothing can be made out of Nothing.*
> William Shakespeare
> *King Lear*

But when it came to laying his money on the Greyhound counter, he could not bring himself to do it. Having the cash in his pocket was a power he did not wish to lose. Rather than stand on the highway where he might meet that sheriff again, he hung out at a trucker's cafe until he cadged a ride east. The trucker, wired and heavily stoned, wanted someone to talk to.

Swallow had been holding long-haul trucking in the back of his mind as a possible career alternative. Spend a lot of time alone, listening to music. See America. The trucker quickly disillusioned him.

—Cost of fuel doubling every month, I'm about to lose my truck. Truck is worth a hundred thousand dollars, with interest rates at fifteen percent, you can do the arithmetic yourself, and I can't make the payments, I'm three payments behind, plus I still owe for fuel clear back to December. And if that's not enough, now we're supposed to be on strike, Parkhurst's *Overdrive* outfit called it, and it's probably right, it's probably the only thing left to try, but I can't strike because I'd lose the one contract I count on to half stay even, hell, they said if I didn't run they'd sue me for default. So now on top of everything else, I'm a scab, and I hear there's blockades in North Carolina, and this little peashooter here ain't much protection if there is.

He flipped back an oil rag by the gearbox to show Swallow a revolver that looked plenty large, but Swallow had to agree that he hoped not to be part of crashing any gypsy trucker blockade lines. The good news was they encountered none, and the greatest danger he had to contend with all the way into Raleigh was the trucker's erotic obsession with Patty Hearst. Hearst, heiress to the great newspaper fortune, had been kidnapped by a wacko radical group, the Symbionese Liberation Army, and then apparently gone over to their cause. On the dashboard of the truck was a photograph taken in April, with Hearst holding a machine gun in a pose the trucker found unbearably exciting, one elegant manicured hand around the barrel, the other curled on the trigger, her shoulders set and her lips clenched in revolutionary determination. All the way across Kentucky, the trucker imagined the lubricity of Hearst's sexual organs. Swallow feigned sleep, then slept, then it was Raleigh, and for the ride up to Richmond he went back to flagging down cars.

The thing I hated most about my mom, I mean, except for her driving away my dad, was her men.

I hated the mere fact that they were in my house. I hated their laughter. The proprietary way they took ownership of the very air, sat at leisure in the best chair surveying their surroundings to see how well they suited.

Ed, the fat red-haired accountant in polo shirts, with his wheezing voice. Gordon of the oily pompadour, who never came out of the bedroom. Steve, beefy, honest Steve, who was always trying to get me out back to throw a football around, who wanted to take the three of us skiing, the worst disaster weekend of my life, motel with the two of them, my mom on the slopes, panicking so bad she pissed on herself in her snowsuit.

Swallow was just another one. For a long time. The cocky damned way he stood. That grin that always made you feel like . . . it wasn't so much that you were stupid, just that you were so obvious.

The things that finally broke through about Swallow:

>Eye contact. He never avoided my gaze.

>He didn't change the way he talked to talk to me.

>He didn't change the way he talked to talk to my mom.

>He didn't let her get weird.

He didn't pretend to be my big buddy, but after he and Mom got regular, he just started hanging out with me as if that were natural, not as if there were any distance to have to be overcome, not as if he were making an effort to do it, not like a campaign, like Steve's campaign. Just when my mom was tired or wanted to watch TV, he'd wrinkle up his face and say

—How 'bout you, Stu, you want to go look for something to do?

Which I always did. And what we did was never something laid out for you to do. I mean, like a movie or bowling or something that exists for the purpose of entertaining. It was always just poking around. Wandering through hardware stores. Visiting old coots. Driving up dirt roads to see what was up them. Or just walking. Up one street and down the other. Comparing houses. Talking about stuff. The loosest collection of stuff. Could be Reinhard Gehlen at the end of World War II, could be the one sure cure for headache. Or what the desert looks like to a lizard. He was always pointing something out. 'Did you see that, Stu?' Some bird, or an erratic rock, or maybe even just the odd shape of the barbs on a rusty string of barbed wire. 'You ever see barbs like that, like little curry combs?'

I don't suppose I let myself know how much my world revolved around him, because of what could never change about my mom and men, but I let go further than, certainly further than I ever did before and probably more than I ever have again to this day.

So when it got skritchy between them, it was really horrible for me. I stopped going home. Would do anything to avoid being where the two of them were.

And when he left I wasn't there.

He found me the next day at school, after school. — I didn't want to leave town without . . . I don't know. I don't want to try to explain. I've never been worth shit at goodbyes.

—Fuck you.

He nodded. —Keep your heart exposed to the weather.

And then he left.

"I delight in Nothing"
Par Lagerkvist
The Dwarf

When he got to Richmond he expected to find T.J. chafing. Instead he found T.J. still helping Linda unpack, helping Linda get her water turned on, helping Linda find a job. Swallow had to cool his own heels for almost a week at friends of Linda's. What started out cutely awkward, his crashing on the couch of three young women, turned just awkward after three days. None of the three women was interested in sleeping with Swallow, but each was on edge that he might prefer one of the others, so the simplest business with toast and jam was tangled in layers of approach-avoidance tension. He spent as much time out of the apartment as he could, saw all the Poe-iana available in Richmond, went crabbing on the Rappahannock, learned to love crepe myrtle trees, and walked the downtown streets looking for androids. He didn't see any. Most of the people were black. He wondered if there were black androids. He wondered what race had to do with it.

At night, T.J. would come over and they would take long walks. T.J. loved long walks, and Linda didn't. Separating from Linda was obviously difficult work. On the long walks, T.J. would talk about how it was going with Linda for about ten minutes, then revert to his standard topic. Way back in art school, T.J. had come to the decision that separating art objects from other objects was an essential mistake, was *the* essential mistake in western civilization, and the right path was to make *every* object an art object. So while Swallow worked on his rice paper paintings, T.J. would turn in sketches for fire plugs, sewer grates, freeway off-ramps. The project kept enlarging, as T.J. realized that one fire plug in a badly designed city was worse than none, and what was necessary was to redesign the whole city to make it suitable for humans. When Swallow moved into the mountains with Blue, he had lost track of the project, and T.J. caught him up now. Following some logic Swallow couldn't quite ken, T.J. had taken an odd turn into retro-fitting nature. Apparently, T.J. had abandoned hope that the human-built environment could be sufficiently changed to make it fit with the biological world, so T.J. was now sketching ideas for altering the biological to give it a chance to survive in the humanosphere. He didn't have his sketchbooks with him, but as they walked, he worked through the concepts for Swallow.

One night, after a meal of very bad pizza—never eat pizza in Richmond, Virginia—Swallow and T.J. stepped out of the pizzeria, the glutinous cheese like molding leather in their bellies. T.J., distracted by a streetlight, began describing the latest additions to his design for the tree as an effective urban organism. They started to cross Twenty-Fifth, with the light. An Olds, turning, jerked to a hard stop, putting a glossier sheen on T.J.'s jeans. Then the driver had the gall to slam a fat hand on his horn.

The boot hit the fender. How can they make a car so heavy, when all the metal has the structural strength of Kleenex? A four-foot section of it crumpled.

A backstroke, with the heel, explosive pop and the tinkle of glass.

The driver was out of his door, red, sweating. —You MANIAC!

Calm, studied, unemotional, T.J. put his boot directly sole forward into a thousand-dollar grill, pushed off and delivered a rising side-kick high on the hood.

—You FREAK! Somebody call the cops!

T.J. studied his work, then turned to the man, stooping to brush glass shards from his jeans. —Go ahead, Charlie. You hit me in the crosswalk. I may be crippled for life. I hope you got a big house, Charlie, because I intend to spend your last penny. On drugs.

He straightened his cuff. —Or else you can drive away.

Swallow had always admired T.J.'s style. The secret, he decided, was that T.J. didn't look challenging. People respond to challenge with belligerence. What T.J. always did was give them a choice and make it clear with every muscle of his face that he didn't care what they chose. Swallow decided T.J. would be a good parent.

The fat man got back in his Olds. Now if it had been me, Swallow thought,

I might holler after him how he should be more careful. But that would be exactly wrong. If you tell somebody what lesson you think they should learn from an experience, all you do is set them up to resist that lesson. What you do, you give them the experience, and the instruction is a natural consequence.

— Piss poor design, said T.J., walking away. Bad enough to drag around this ton of metal everywhere you want to ship a human being, and the exhaust, and the land use. But crossing them with pedestrian traffic? Cars kill a pedestrian every three hours, and cripple a kid every seventeen minutes. Doesn't anyone ever think at all?

The sky was bright and sunny, the air thin, cold. The ground beneath our boots was frozen mud, snowless, sculpted still in the flowing motions of the last thaw. I'll never forget that irregular, hard, temporary ground—how like it this all is.

I had never seen morale in our band so low. On the surface, it did not show. There were no knifings. Whisky rations were standard. You could see it, though, in the faces, whiter and somehow too thin. You could hear it in the voices, in the edge the voices held even at the friendliest. You could feel it in the quickness of reactions, alertness of hearing, intensity of stares.

I had backed the band across sixteen shifts, each time pretending to advance. It had been months since our last contact with forces hostile or allied. Each shift was to a place more alien. Each called for more harsh work, each offered fewer creature comforts. The last six had afforded not the slightest chance of relaxation. I knew, and I knew they knew, that the next several would be yet more intense, while yet less encouraging.

I tell you, and I ask you to believe me now, it was all necessary.

No one on the forty acres would work with his grandfather, so it fell to Swallow. Swallow actually liked his grandfather. His grandfather had played games with him since he was barely able to figure out how the checkers would hop. His grandfather spent most of his time sitting under large trees, sitting still for hours, without saying a word. No one else on the property could sit still, no one else was ever quiet. But sometimes he got up from his metal chair beneath the elms, filled up his wheelbarrow, which he used as a tool crib, with crow bar, staple puller, hammer, and coffee cans full of nails and staples, and Swallow would have to go with him, down into the pasture, to fix the fences. The fences always seemed to always need fixing.

By then the suburbs had grown up, and the kids in those new houses were kids Swallow had to go to school with, kids whose aerospace engineer families had just moved in from New Jersey to work at the big rocket plant south of town, kids who had grown up in suburbs, dressed better, talked faster, made friends faster, and knew what was cool. Swallow didn't want to go out to the fence line where the kids in those houses could see him with his old coot grandfather, with his rusty old wheelbarrow, prying on rusty old barbed wire. Swallow's grandfather made him wear a hat and gloves, the hat an old man's Stetson, the gloves as big as the wheelbarrow.

All the barbed wire was ancient. There were seventeen kinds of it behind his grandfather's garage, each with differently shaped barbs, like letters in some unknown alphabet. When a piece of fence broke, Swallow's grandfather would twist another piece onto it. He would loosen staples on the creaky wooden posts—well, not really posts, rickety dry tree limbs, half of them—loosen the staples at least four posts back from the break, so he could stretch the wire tight. He'd stretch with the crowbar, pulling it tighter and tighter while it creaked and cracked. It was just face high to Swallow, and sometimes it did break again, flash out right at him.

When the wire was tight, they stapled it to the posts. The staples, too, were used, used many times, rusted red, needing to be hammered straight before being used once more. In the giant gloves, Swallow would always drop the staple. Swallow's grandfather would swear in some border half-Spanish. The staple had no point, so hammering it in was like hammering a spoon. Good thing the posts were so soft it was like hammering a spoon into a stick of butter. Everything tasted like dust, and the whole time Swallow knew the kids in those new houses could see him.

Each day I get my wife off to work. Which is never just easy, it always involves some flurry, tension, a hundred last-minute questions, and usually at least one coming back for something she has forgotten. When she is finally gone, the house gets quiet, and when that quiet sinks in, I go downstairs to the home theater. Which I suppose I should start calling something else. Nowadays, 'home theatre' makes people think of expensive electronic devices for watching pixels of light, sub-woofers to help out with the sounds of explosions. My home theatre is a stage six feet deep and fifteen feet wide, floored with unfinished fir and illuminated by spotlights made from old half-gallon coffee cans painted black. There are no seats for an audience. (I suppose it is unnecessary to say that there is no audience.) I take off my sweater, turn on the spotlights, and take the stage.

I pick up where I left off in a serial drama involving a large cast of characters. I play all the parts. Because the script (which I suppose is it unnecessary to say exists only in my head) is so rough, I need to go repeatedly back over scenes to try to get them right. The morning is usually spent repeating scenes from yesterday's work. If the afternoon is good, we get some new scenes.

When the production is a road musical, which involves a great deal of singing and dancing, I am usually physically exhausted by the end of the day. But that is good exhaustion, unlike the mental fatigue that comes from the tightly knotted conflicts in one of those clotted dramas with characters circling one another like bantam fighting snakes, conflicts never resolved, never even heightened into any clarity, only progressively revealed to be deeper and more oblique than originally presented. Frequently the characters are cruel to one another in ways that leave me with injuries. Or worse, it could be the Swallow stuff.

My wife returns at the point of highest drama. I quickly switch off the spotlights, slip my sweater back on, and dash up the stairs to meet her at the door. She tells me about her day, long descriptions of everything experienced, felt, and said by peripheral characters I have never met. What they thought about it all. Then, at some point, she pauses and asks me how my day went.

> *Nothing succeeds like success.*
> *Folk Wisdom*

Swallow read the cartoon strip on the ride up to New York in T.J.'s Datsun. He liked it. It was called 'The Last Man on Earth.' It was set in the near future, after the global apocalypse. The visitors from the Intergalactic Sentients Association show up exactly a week too late. All they find is rubble and one stunned and hungry survivor. So they probe him about what humans were like. The comedy is in his replies, and in their misunderstandings.

> ISA creature with 17 eyes: I'll never understand this thing you call humor or what it's used for.
>
> Last Man on Earth: We live a meaningless existence in a pointless universe. Humor is what gives us hope, life, and joy.
>
> ISA creature: But you laugh at such hopeless, lifeless, joyless things!
>
> Last Man on Earth: That's no hopeless, lifeless, joyless thing. That's my wife.

Satire is essentially a matter of perspective. Swallow thought T.J. had found a pretty good perspective. The syndicate didn't. T.J. went directly there, even before Lang's apartment. He knew people there by name, they'd invited the submission, they were primed for the concept, but they turned the strip down flat. —No character. There's no one for the reader to identify with. You want an Everyman.

—What's more Everyman than the last man on Earth?

—What does it have to do with my morning coffee? Here. Here's one we just signed. Take it home and bring me back one like that.

They handed him a six-week run of a new strip called Garfield. Garfield was a cat. A fat, unpleasant cat, whose main characteristics were gluttony and aggression. In the first panel Garfield sees a chocolate cake. In the second panel he eats it. In the third panel he licks his chops. In the fourth he says 'If only dogs were made of chocolate.'

— But it's not funny. It's just crude.

—It gives people permission to be crude. They need it. They're tired of being ashamed of it. You want to argue or you want to learn? You want a strip? Draw me Richard Nixon as a rat. Cute rat, round up his nose, give him a cute tail. He plots and schemes and all his motivation is base and transparent.

—A hundred editorial cartoonists do that every day.

—But they disapprove! Don't disapprove. Everybody has a little bit of Nixon. Show me my Nixon so I can see it without shame.

—That's disgusting.

—That's therapeutic. Go back and reread your Chaucer. What you want, T.J., you want to be a judge. You want to show the reader his insides and then condemn him. The reader doesn't need that. He wants you to give him permission.

—Thanks, Michael. I need a couple weeks to think about this.

—And don't draw so fancy. Draw simple. Draw fast. The reader can spot art with his eyes half-closed. No art and no big words. Monosyllables and fat lines. A cute rat, in fat lines. Bring me that.

In the elevator down, T.J. agreed that Michael was right. Swallow was outraged. How could T.J. just cave in like that? —There's a purpose to condemnation. Righteousness has its place. This self-help shit has gone too far. These self-serving little assholes already give themselves too much permission to be vain and greedy and shallow and self-centered. And nasty. Ignorant. Did I say shallow? God, have you ever been to Newport Beach? The last thing they need is to be told it's cute. You need to make them vomit. You need to make them wake in the night in a cold sweat and have to get up and go into the living room and brew tea and sit shaking for hours. That's what they need. It's not cute.

L.A.Heberlein

—But he's right. You can't be superior. Who wants holier than thou?

—I do. I'm starved for someone to admire. Jeez, you go to the movies, and there's no one with any values you can look up to. The way Woody could look up to Bogie. Who could anybody look up to now? The most attractive thing you could offer a needy readership is a moral center. I think that Michael is an android. And he's wrong about Chaucer.

—Chaucer was pretty jolly. Chaucer was pretty accepting.

—Chaucer attacked simony more bitterly than Martin Luther did. He didn't think it was funny. He didn't think it was cute.

—Yeah, but all the fart jokes, and how everyone's a lecher.

—Sure. Lechery is human and you accept it. Farts are human and they're funny. Simony is a betrayal and you expose it, and when you expose it you don't want the priests to feel accepted and forgiven.

—I don't know, man. I'm starting to give up on connecting with an audience. I don't think they want to hear it. Maybe I should go back to my trees.

I was teaching American literature at a university in the mountain West. Okay, it was the University of Montana. It was a one-year contract. It didn't get renewed. I lived forty-five minutes from town up a steep canyon. At the end of the year, I invited all my students up for a going-away party. I baked a turkey, a salmon, and a ham. I brought home a whole Jeep load of beer. I even filled a goldfish bowl full of pre-rolled joints. Hell, I was already fired, what were they going to do?

Of 120-some current students, only four made it up the canyon that day. One was this strong-jawed, well-muscled fraternity guy who always seemed to enjoy it when I came into class incoherent after speeding all night. God knows why he was at the party. Maybe he thought he could bring home more stories to tell. Then there were two young women. Carol and Valerie. They were friends. Carol was chubby and laughed a lot. I always looked forward to reading her papers. My assignments always started, 'Write on anything you want. If you don't have any ideas, here are some.' Every student that whole year chose one of the topics I suggested, except Carol. She would write on something so obliquely related to the subject at hand that maybe it wasn't, even. Three deft touches to show that she'd read the book, heard my lectures, understood the book, understood my lectures, had a handle on that whole situation, and then she was off on her own tangent. Which was quirky and weird and completely obscure. Valerie was a friend of hers. The fourth student that came was Valerie's boyfriend. For the life of me, I can't remember his name.

I made a complete fool of myself trying to keep them all from leaving, after they'd stayed a polite spell. I railed at them, I tried to bribe them. Finally Carol had to make fun of me, mimic me in my own kitchen, and even then, though I was ashamed of how I was acting, I didn't want to let them go. It was as though demons were lurking in the pines outside, and when the last guest left I would be slowly dismembered.

Probably also I was making a fool of myself over Valerie. I don't know how anybody else does it. I mean, be a guy and teach young women. Maybe there's a mental trick to it. Like I knew someone once who worked in a bank, and she said it got fairly quickly so that it wasn't even like it was money they were handling, it was just this green paper. I suppose for good teachers it's like that. They understand the role of trust in which they have been placed, and they respect it so much that they don't even see their female students that way. Me, it just threw me completely off my rails, every time I went into a classroom and all those young women looked up at me, this sea of budding faces. And, of every one of those faces that year, Valerie's was the most amazing. I had failed as a teacher and was leaving that town, and so probably I was trying to pretend I wasn't hoping that at the end of the giant party I had planned, finally, after a year of cold sweats and trying not to stare, one of those women would come to my house and let me touch her. Especially if it was Valerie.

And, this is how obtuse I am, probably all four of those students realized all this then, thirty years ago, could instantly scan what is just slowly appearing to me now. And no wonder they fought to escape my increasingly deranged harangues. Escape they did. On the way out, Valerie's boyfriend, whatever his name was, waved a spiral notebook at me. —I thought maybe you might find this interesting.

I didn't look at it. I guess I packed it in the box with my lecture notes. And would you believe I still have them? After all those cross-country moves. They were still in the same liquor-store box I put them in when I packed up that house up that canyon in Montana. When my daughter, whose specialty is the medieval lyric, got her first tenure-track job, at a small university in the South, they threw a varied load at her. Composition of course, but also two survey courses. Once an over-helpful dad, always an over-helpful dad, and I thought my old lecture notes might at least amuse her, maybe even provide some jumping-off points.

In the box of lecture notes was the spiral notebook, which I had never opened. And in that spiral notebook was this book, in a spidery hand. The ascenders and descenders were extremely elongated, and the little letters so small as to be difficult to decipher. Several colors of ink had been used. The main line of the Swallow story, the story of Swallow's trip from Colorado to Chicago, Virginia, New York, North Carolina, Puerto

Escondido, and home, was written in a pale blue. Most of the bits in which a narrator addresses the reader directly to explain the point were red. Other first-person narration was usually conducted in a distinctive sharp green. The Gray story, about the Fire, was in jet black. The little snippets that seemed to imply alternate universes were a variety of colors, primarily brown. But the color-coding, if that is what it in fact was, was not consistent or schematic. The Chicago episode was a patchwork of various inks, and the little snippet of Diane and T.J. was in Swallow's blue. I don't think the color scheme is central to an understanding of how the pieces fit together, but I believe the pieces do fit together. Of course, as we know, the human mind seeks pattern and coherence when there is none, hence the widespread belief in astrology and conspiracy theories. It is possible that some of the matter is extraneous. But I think the pieces were intended to form a coherent whole, and I can convince myself that I see the connections, most of them at least.

The kid, so far as I remember him—and, you know, I was barely conscious of the male students in my classrooms—was undistinguished, did the work but never showed any originality or spirit. He was so thin that if he were female you would immediately assume anorexia. A shock of scrawny chocolate-colored hair came straight down into his eyes, and he was forever flipping it aside. I think maybe he usually wore a down jacket. After I read the spiral notebook, I made some effort to find him. I had kept a couple of Carol's papers, because they were so funny, so I had her last name. I tried looking her up on Classmates.com, and places like that. No trace.

I have to admit that I also thought maybe she could fill me in on what had become of Valerie.

Man is the only one that knows Nothing.
Pliny the Elder

Where they went was Lang's apartment. Lang was talking to two friends, a guy with an incredible haircut and a woman with an impeccable British accent. Lang milked the opportunity to play sophisticated New Yorker to Swallow and T.J.'s country rubes. Lang had been in New York almost a year. He crammed every sentence full of local referents, forcing the interlocutor from the country to say, What's that? Where's that? Who's that?

—And then we stopped on the way home to see Margaret Pageler at the Crumbling Cornice.

Then, when you were forced to ask 'Who's Margaret Pageler?' he wouldn't just say who Margaret Pageler was, he'd stop cold, turn slowly towards you, and say, 'Oh, you've never heard of Margaret Pageler?'

Swallow stopped playing. There was nothing to eat in the apartment, Lang adamant that bringing any food into the building would bring roaches and hence the wrath of all the neighbors, it was the most anti-social thing you could do. Swallow poked around the tiny room trying to ignore the conversation. Big window facing the street. Little kitchen in back. Above it Lang's bedroom and bath, the bath the only thing new, the rest of the apartment still looking nineteenth century and as though it had not been painted since, the floors wavy and rough like the floors of a barn, the plumbing exposed and corroding. But the bath looked like the dressing room for a soap opera star. There were seven mirrors, four of them different grades of high magnification, so looking at your skin you saw huge pores with grease in them like the grease on that pizza in Richmond. You could learn more than you wanted to know about the shape and structure of follicles. In the bedroom Swallow found a typescript of Lang's novel. Lang's novel was about a twenty-two-year-old retired coke dealer. Lang was a twenty-two-year-old retired coke dealer. The retired twenty-two-year-old coke dealer in the novel had to come out of retirement to rescue an innocent friend from a South American prison. Every noun in every sentence had exactly two adjectives in front of it. *She stopped at the top of the long, oaken stairway and brushed her silky, auburn hair with a stiff, white brush.*

Lang's friends finally left, and Lang tried to convince them that the woman was Johanna, from 'Visions of Johanna.'

—He wrote it about her. She was living in the loft next door that winter. He used to come over. They never slept together. She was just kind of this vision of an alternative to his actual domestic life.

Swallow thought about Diane. Diane in Morrison, sitting on the highway guardrail throwing rocks into Bear Creek. He was trying to sit close to her. He could smell her hair. Her hair smelled like towels when you take them off the clothesline on a hot day.

—You know, you could fly, she said. Did you know that?

—Lord, I try.

—No, I mean really fly. If you just let go, very still with your eyes shut, and just lifted, you could come right off the ground.

Years later, alone on a bench at a bus stop, he would find himself squeezing his eyes and tugging upwards, trying to make his body light.

Later that afternoon she tried to talk him into driving her to Washington. She wanted to burn herself on the steps of the Pentagon. She had her father's credit card, for the gasoline.

He remembered Cin, in Taos. They've been married a little over a year. It's an ugly apartment in what had probably been a storefront in the thirties. The walls are painted yellow. He's lying on a concrete floor, has been there for hours. The ceiling is pipes and peeling. He is crying out of one eye.

It's the left eye, not puffy, not reddened, just emitting water, the whole left side of his shirt soggy from it. No sobbing, no noise at all, and no feeling. Only that one eye crying as hard as it knows how.

The sound of a key in a lock, then of tumblers turning, the ill-cut door forced open, her keys clattering on the Formica table.

—Tuke?

He didn't answer, and then she was above him, tall and strange from the strange perspective. She knelt down, ran her fingers through his hair, was gone, then back, with a barely damp washcloth, sponging his wet side.

She kissed her index finger and put it to his lips, then sponged the rest of his face. —When you need someone, I'm here.

He listened for a long time to her move about the apartment, humming with the little radio, then he got up and made his way like a cat to her in the kitchen. He put his arms around her waist and hid his face in the back of her neck. She put down the knife and turned to him. He kissed her on the forehead.

They ate dinner curled together on the concrete floor, not speaking.

I met Janis Joplin in July of 1967 in San Francisco. I had done the closest thing I could to running away to San Francisco: negotiated a peace with my parents, arranged to stay with a friend of my mother's, who was an anthropology professor at Berkeley. The first night in her apartment, as I was going from the shower to the guest room, she was sitting cross-legged on the floor of the den in a kimono smoking black hash. She asked if I wanted a toke. From then on it was all cool. I could stay out all night, and if she asked questions, it was out of the same sort of curiosity a peer would exhibit.

I met Janis on the street in the Fillmore district. I was sixteen and skinny and untutored, fresh from the country, just the way she liked them. She took me up to her room and I did everything she said. When we were exhausted she hit up and poured us each a drink and then she asked me to leave.

I wanted to stay. I tried to tell her. —I can be there for you, in the night. I can make a difference.

Her voice—her voice was lonelier than a freight train's horn sounding miles away at night in the country. You could feel all the hurt in it, all through you. The America I grew up in was all about shiny plastic and a fake smile. Janis Joplin's voice was the first true thing I'd ever encountered in that America. The singers who had come before were about show business, about stage, about pretend. Janis was about what it really felt like being human. And what it really felt like hurt so bad you would never get over it. It was being alive, and being alive was pain, old, deep, and never to be gotten over. I don't care what they teach you in schools and in church, that voice says, I don't care what the ads say on TV, here is how it hurts to be alive. Just a few notes of that voice, from a car radio turning a corner a block away, will still freeze me in my steps, and I'll have to stop whatever I was doing and re-evaluate my whole life, everything I'd been running around doing as though it had any importance at all in the larger scheme of things. This blue that runs right through your blood down into the center of the earth, that has been there since long before your kind. One of her wordless rising wails, where the voice splits in two as it rises, pauses, and then drives nails right through you.

I still wake up sometimes thinking I could have saved her. There she was, and there I was. If I had only been able to think of what to say, what to be. I could have been what she needed. If only I had enough *substance* to fill the hole inside her. America's greatest cultural resource, lost to my inadequacy.

Instead I came home from San Francisco in the fall, went back to high school, as though the Summer of Love had not happened, as though America had not cracked down the middle and a new creation upwelled from the exposed hot core. Then off to art school, where I met Cindy and dated her as though it were the 1950's.

Gray sipped from a cup of bitter tea and stretched his back. He was home from a week-long deep-space party, and one night's corporeal sleep had come nowhere near regenerating him fully. He ached. His head was a ball of fuzz. Give a man a fresh body, perfectly-engineered, tuned, balanced, and adjusted, and in ten minutes he'll have his lesions, burns, and traumatic contusions projected into every cell of it. Gray had only been in the body overnight, and already it tasted of metal, like old rusty wire left coiled behind a barn in the rain. Remembering the detached, cool taste of the void, Gray sipped the tea slowly, letting it cool in the air and on the skin of his mouth in small takes, tasting each trickle with all of his tongue, swallowing in even unhaste.

On the rough pine kitchen table lay spread a good three reams of high gloss paper covered with sketches and computations, radiation-line breakdowns for a visual design system. The sketches were years old. Gray had done them in college and had tried half-heartedly to sell the idea ever since. The breakdowns and computations were new. Eight months ago, when he had come back from the Fire, he had put a push on and had sold the design to Inca Atmospherics. Inca had given him a working budget that was almost all he had asked for; now it was more than exhausted. Projectors surrounded his world, wired into the spaghetti mess of a prototype control board in the other room, but none of the computations and breakdowns on enamel paper were more than a quarter finished, and he hadn't even started the schematics. Gray knew exactly what he wanted of each unit; it was only a matter of spending hours and days filling in the specifics. Gray had been putting off that drudgery ever since he got funded, preferring to fiddle with fine-tuned omnichromatic mists which weren't included in the Inca design, and to record program after program of new arrangements which he played out continually on his prototype while he sat on the long porch in back, rocking in an ion-suspension frame chair and cuddling the huge cat on his lap.

L.A.Heberlein

He got up from the table now, poured himself a very tall glass of pear juice, walked to the porch and got into the rocker. Old Cat was nowhere around. Gray turned on the system and watched while the sky went warm from its soft gray-black. There was a serious light leak on the far north horizon, and a small crackle and sputter out over the ocean. It was a bother, but no serious problem, only a matter of finding the faulty relays inside. It couldn't be the projectors. They were good units supplied by Inca themselves. It was somewhere inside, probably in the monitor, possibly just a feedback problem in the final gain. He would find it eventually when he got to the schematic recordings. He would probably find a lot of things if he ever got to the schematics.

He sat back in the rocker and keyed a tape onto the system, a simple self-modulating abstract expressionist arrangement, with centers in lightning blue around the zenith. It was a good arrangement, Gray thought, but when he had cut the tape, a high-frequency noise had got through the filters, causing the iceberg pinwheels to blur occasionally and to splatter a little. He sat in the rocker and watched it play out, wondering where Old Cat was. If he could cut several more tapes like the one he had on, maybe he could use them as demos when he gave the system to Inca. Maybe he could use that in to find a way to get the tapes released professionally. He could cut tapes for home use, maybe even work it into a chance to play live in small clubs. From clubs, there was a shot at finding his way into a deep-space group. Deep space, Gray handling deep-space controls, playing on deep-space images. It could happen. Other people had done it.

He spent the morning on the back porch, watching his world run, the stable valleys and canyons spreading down before him old and purple in quiet, cool breezes, sky moving to his music, cool, relaxed. At noon he went up into the windowed loft of the cabin and ate strawberries, peaches, blackberries and cream. The strawberries were slightly green, and the warranty on the food unit had long since expired. Getting the unit serviced would cost as much as buying a new one. Perhaps he could find a fix-it-yourself book; it was probably simply a matter of replacing one judgment board. Gray knew he wouldn't get around to fixing it. Maybe he could sell it when he moved. It would be a hassle to move it anyway. Gray wanted to move as soon as he finished the Inca project. The sky on this place was too small for any professional work. If he moved into an older place, maybe a bit rundown, without many furnishings, in a worse neighborhood, he could get maybe a doubling of the horizon, a big increase in canopy size, and some depth of field for his projectors, without any increase in rent. He didn't have all that much love for bourgeois conveniences in the first place, and many of his friends were starting to move down into the more populated areas anyway; he'd be closer to things. An artistic community was developing along the Upper Sandleston. He could move there. It was an old area with huge old homes, that had once been very fine places, and if they weren't so fine now, they were still very large. Maybe he could even move in with someone and split the rent. It would be hard to share a place, but a man must after all make decisions about priorities, and Gray knew he needed a decent-sized canopy to work on.

He grabbed a handful of gingerknich seeds and went downstairs to his control board to check the mailbox. The power company, in a single composite message, informed him his rates had been increased pursuant to the decision of some regulatory agency it probably owned, advised him to decrease power usage, especially during peak periods, to avoid further temporary shortages, advertised its latest service availabilities, and demanded immediate payment on a long overdue bill. There were three newspapers and several magazines. Lots of bills: from Spivak's for generator color masters he had already worn down, from the subscription department of one of the magazines, from Standard Transportation's revolving charge plan. Several phone messages, but only three from today—Taylor at Inca, and then Jelly Cornfish twice. Gray flipped the phone from record to ring and answer, but he didn't return the calls.

Gray then knocked about the cabin for a little, absentmindedly eating gingerknich seeds, dropping more on the floor than got into his mouth, and leafing through the magazines. His knocking about took him, eventually, up to the elevated mosaic courtyard which could have been called his workroom or studio. He continued knocking about there, picking up an occasional loose object sitting in the wrong place and carrying it around with him like a worry stone, forgetting he had it, then unconsciously setting it down someplace even more irrational than the place he had found it. If it were something like an alligator clip, a writing implement, or a minor relay, chances were good it would be twisted apart, into some meaningless, convoluted shape when he set it down. When he had come out, he had switched on a small table radio, with the little speakers built into the mosaic patio; now he was thinking for the millionth time that what he missed most about his home in Crystal City was Dumptruck O'Neil's afternoon radio show. There wasn't another station like Dumptruck's anywhere else in the universe.

Gray eventually—this is the way it always worked—found himself knocking about in front of the board. And eventually he decided he might get more done afterwards if he relaxed awhile on his instrument. So he picked up a keyboard in each hand and ran a lead down each of the bony fingers of his new corporeal home. He reached up to the board and shut off the tape that was playing, shut off the background-normal lighting system that kicked on when the tape was turned off, and he stood for a minute in the thick blackness of night, no light anywhere in the sky. He began keying some simple folk rhythms and gradually added harmony lines, thin, hard, fading tracers of colors like cobalt blue and candy-apple maroon. There were too many of them; he cut them back, and then again, until they were only distant isolated arcs cutting the sky, far apart from each other. It was a satisfying rhythm section, even though he could not bring up the presence of the snapping lines as well as he would have liked, given the equipment he had. He considered turning on a console recorder to take notes from if he decided to use something later, but he didn't. He had spool after spool of him diddling already, and enough half-finished real programs so that he wasn't looking for ideas. He stepped out into the center of the floor and began keying simple chords against the basic rhythm.

They fell into a pattern he had learned from a friend when he was just a boy, an easy, repetitive pattern he usually found himself playing when he wasn't thinking, when he had no greater arrangement to work within, simple syncopated changes just off the beat, a repetition of two changes, varied endlessly—he could forget complex picking styles and larger structures and work with the same simple figure, bending and reversing and phasing until he had established a certain atmosphere within his own mind, or developed a variation which emerged as a theme, or both, or neither, and then slide into the next chord in the simple progression that was one of the first he had ever learned, and work within it the same way. He had spent years within that progression. It was his and it was comfortable. It did not have the drive and structure of an arrangement, it was useless for performance, the type of self-centered piece that could never mean much to anyone not actually wrapped up inside it and using its simplicity to think with.

Gray wondered for a moment whether real arrangers had reached the state where they could do something similar with real pieces, get so comfortable they could think inside them. It was possible they could. If you could master the complicated mechanics of performance pieces so well that they became as much a part of your nervous system as a simple progression does, perhaps you could be right inside them. Maybe you could live there. Gray admired the possibility until his harmonic variations degenerated into rhythmless hunting for color. He set his rhythm back up and moved rapidly all the way through the progression and back to where he had been, then settled back down into the spot he knew there.

He was standing awkwardly in his corporeal skin, bent over, his hands bent inward in front of his lower chest. There was no way he could stand that let him feel comfortable. Rigid, he felt his body was not a part of what his mind was doing. It confirmed his already deep belief in the uselessness of the body. No dance he had ever seen, no motion he had ever produced, had ever possessed any real grace, had ever seemed more than a parody of the grace he had seen in other human creations, had ever risen above the level of contrived, pretentious show.

Gray wondered what it would be like to play in deep space, with nothing but pure cerebral power.

He was hitting hard and even on the elemental changes now, slow, but very firm, forsaking the teasing pleasure of subtle variation for the firmity and distance-pull of straight, simple repetition, again, again. Playing, he walked, almost drifted, to the control board and stomped twice on the foot switch that controlled final gain. The sky leapt out at him, colors exploding toward him, way closer, the whole arrangement suddenly right on top of him. Then it fuzzed with sheer presence and all the definition dropped off sharply, intensity lost in the distortion. Gray shut it off, shut it all off, even the background rhythms, until it was still and foggy black again. There isn't a whole lot else you can do when a lower intensity won't satisfy you and your amplifiers won't put out more. As he sat in the darkness, the tinny radio, playing some banal popular tune, intruded on his consciousness. Irritated, he snapped it off. With it off, he heard the phone ringing.

It was Jelly Cornfish. She invited herself over. He said okay. When he picked up the keyboards again, he didn't turn on a rhythm section or start one of his comfortable progressions. Instead he tried to work an exercise from a book. He played through the exercise over and over again, awkward and making mistakes. He hauled out the exercise book from where he had it hidden beneath magazines, embarrassed that someone might see it, and he tried a second scale. He tried to arch the nerves and veins and muscles in the back of his fingers back to form the first image in the scale, but he could not reach even the first note. He stood there aching and reaching, straining against the inelasticity of his reflexes, the sky above him flickering blurrily around approximations of a clean, delicate shape. After a long time he gave up, ran once again, fumblingly, through the first scale, then switched on the rhythm section and played once again with his old, familiar chords.

Growing quickly bored, he unwired himself, put a hollow blue on the sky, and went back to the kitchen. He pulled one sheaf of the papers toward him. He was being paid to design an economical home playback system that could compete with currently available models, not to hunker over a keyboard pretending he was a deep-space star. He had a deadline, and if he worked straight through beginning right now, he still did not have time to do it right.

It took him some time to find his place, to get himself inside the additive connections, to feel once again the place of the part in the whole. He read figures for a long time, then began, slowly, to write some, keying them into a simulator, testing, correcting, pushing the record button once every few minutes in temporary satisfaction, then plunging ahead with the greater problem. It was simple work. He did it almost automatically. It wasn't bad once you got into it. The design stretched out before him. He could see it all. It was a simple matter of staying at it, step by step.

He had only really begun to move ahead when the chimes announced Jelly in the garage, coming in.

From every aspect Nothing is perfect.
Horace
Book II, Ode 16

Lang talked until almost sunup. The next day T.J. was sick. T.J. lay on the couch and groaned while Swallow visited museums. The next day T.J. was sick again, and Swallow met a woman at MOMA. Marla. T.J. was sick for a week. Marla lived in Larchmont, in a three-story house, amazing house of the sort Swallow didn't even know existed, artifact of another race, whose poor country cousins built Cindy's house in Oak Park. Old money hiring old craftsmen. Marla's ex-husband's family, who all thought she was a tramp from the get-go, and now she had the family house. Marla looked like she'd stepped out of a Modigliani. She was self-conscious about her stretch marks and wanted to be reassured about them. She was older than Swallow and had been a schoolteacher until, well she wasn't explicit, but she seemed to be suggesting that she had been romantically involved with a student.

Maybe, Swallow decided after two days, this was why all the books and magazines and movies and songs are all about sex. He had never felt it like this. It was . . . it was that he felt felt by her. When he kissed her, it was that he could feel her lips feeling his lips feeling her lips. It was that he felt he didn't feel anything she didn't feel. It was waves and crests and fountains and pounding surf, explosions and still epiphanies. He kept his eyes about seven inches from hers and locked in on what she was seeing. He had had no idea he had so much energy. He had not known he could scream so loud, or breathe so deeply, or come so hard. He had never passed out before, except from drink. He had never rushed before, except from drugs. He had never shared anything in his life. Now his heart was pounding as though he was just about to OD on life itself, and he felt that both their organisms had broken wide open and were pouring the juices of their life out into a common pool where they would be blended forever. He remembered cartoon scenes of characters spinning round and round and round and round and round. Was that Cinderella, who spun like that?

Her two children were in school until two-thirty each day, when he'd go back into the city, sympathize a bit with T.J., walk around the Village, eat dinner, then go back out to Larchmont.

As miraculous as the sex was, as if God had decided to smile upon them personally and hand them the key to the penthouse where usually only angels got to play, Swallow was even more taken by the transportation system. The BMT to the IRT to Grand Central and the Pelham local. It was beautiful, cheap, fast, thrilling. Nowadays humans couldn't even maintain a transportation system like this, but once upon a time they were able to build it. He marveled at the tile work in the subway stations. He ran his hands over the shining steel cars. He loved the speed. He loved the freedom. He loved not parking. To be able to travel from your apartment, all the way across a state, without a car! One night he made perfect connections, stepping off each train onto the next. He had never been so thrilled.

The last night, counseling at Marianne's, Swallow was somewhat teary. Cindy was distracted, a little angry because she felt guilty, guilty because she couldn't work up enough feeling about the occasion.

– I guess we shouldn't schedule another? Cindy said.

Swallow shook his head.

– It's over, Marianne said.

Marianne had said that two weeks before, when Swallow had been expressing his grief, howling, clutching his sides, crying out. – That's right, Dal. It's over, she had said.

– You don't think we're acting crazy? Cindy asked.

– I always hate to make predictions. This is as clear as I've ever felt, though. You're making the right decision. Now. Is there anything you need to say to each other? Any books that you want to try one more time to close?

Swallow had some trouble talking. —I'm sorry. I'm really sorry. I'm sorry about the abortion. I'm sorry about holding out on you. I'm sorry I never let you in.

Marianne addressed Cindy. – Can you see that he really is sorry?

Cindy nodded.

– Can you forgive him?

Cindy stiffened in the way she stiffened when you made a demand on her, a demand that always made her feel like a bad person, because a good person could have felt what you were trying to get her to feel. —I don't know what that means. When people talk about forgiveness, I don't understand the concept. I don't know what it means.

—Okay. Not forgiveness. Some acceptance?

—I don't know what to accept. I accept that he feels sorry. I'm sorry, too.

—Do you have anything like that to tell Dal?

Cindy went away for a while, then said, no longer angry but sounding direct and sincere: —I'm sorry about trying to stop him from painting.

Swallow looked into her eyes and felt something there that he had missed keenly for years. Of course, then she couldn't stand it, and she started talking about how she didn't succeed in stopping him from painting, he'd just started doing it in secret, and how she'd been careful to make him promise up front that he wasn't an artist, that she didn't want to get involved with any more artists, and was it her fault if he lied about it, but she let that die down fairly quickly, and it didn't take away what had been, that moment when he could look at her and know that she was sorry too.

—About the work we've done here. Anything to say about that?

Then Marianne followed her own question. —I can say that I feel really good about it. I didn't think I was going to. I didn't think you were going to give me a way in. Dal, you were going to keep coming in, doing everything on the surface to smother me with cooperation, and underneath it the total refusal. Just like you gave Mommy, just like you gave Cindy. And Cindy, you were set up not to hear anything from me at all without feeling criticized. It was your finding a stance that broke through it. Dal, you owe that to Cindy. She broke through it for you, too. That night when she said 'I'm not going to take it any more,' that broke through all your ways of not seeing and not hearing, and you'll always owe Cindy that.

—I'll never be able to not see again, Swallow said.

Marianne nodded. — While we're at it, I wanted to thank you. Being with you, seeing you feel that, when you saw what what you'd been doing and what you'd been doing had been doing, made me rethink a lot of things in my own marriage. I think I really changed some things because of that, and I wanted to thank you.

Swallow realized he had not known she was married. He knew nothing about her. She was just someone he used to stand for what was going on inside himself. As he used everyone. But she was paid for that. She was a professional. And she was good. He had never once felt that she didn't understand him, and now when she mentioned herself for the first time he had no difficulty understanding her. —It's a real object lesson, isn't it? he said. You see it good once and you say, 'I can never ever be that way again.'

Cindy looked at them as though she didn't know what they were talking about, the way she looked at people when she thought they were only pretending to be talking about something for the purpose of excluding her.

Marianne spread her palms. —And what's left unfinished? What didn't we do?

Cindy answered. —We never figured out how to have good sex.

—To put that in the singular, Swallow said, I never found my sexuality.

Marianne smiled. —To find your sexuality, you're going to have to give up vengeance. That's how you'll find your sexuality. You're going to have to give up vengeance.

He brewed her some tea and she said she liked it, even though he knew she could not feel the very faint pull and tang in the taste. She complained about how she felt and then went into a laborious and thorough analysis of the current emotional state of everyone she knew. Gray half listened while trying to keep punching an occasional figure into the recorder. It didn't work. He finally shut it off and pushed the papers back into a stack, gave Jelly and himself each another cup of the fine tea, begrudging the cup he was wasting on her, and decided if there was no way to shut off her talk he could at least get her off the subject of other people's dramas.

—Are you still living at home?

She nodded violently. —But I've got my own living area, Steven, I can go days without seeing my parents.

—I bet they still keep track of your comings and goings.

—You should see the fights.

— Why don't you move out?

—Not everyone has your kind of money, Steven.

At that he laughed. —Sheeeeit. The power company told me this morning they were going to shut me off if I didn't pay, and I'm in hock for something like twenty grand to Inca for expenses already gone, and I've got that much more on credit with no way to cover it, and *if* I ever finish up this project, and *if* they decide to go into production on the design, and *if* it sells, I *might* make enough after taxes to pay my back rent. *Maybe*. That's the best I can hope for, if I pull it off and everything works perfectly. To come out stone broke, without a penny to my name.

—Everybody's broke, Steven, she whined. It's just that some people are rich broke and others are okay broke, and some people are poor broke.

He wished he had let her talk about her friends' dramas. — Please, Tish, don't go into your poor little poor girl routine on me this one time, will you?

She sat back and tried to look adult. —Okay, tell me, how much did that tea cost you?

—Do you have to relate everything back to money? This is a clear, faint tea. Can't you appreciate that, can't you appreciate *anything* in the universe, without always looking on the back to see the price tag?

—You can only do that when the price tag doesn't matter.

He just looked at her. He looked his best 'Jelly-I'm-a-broke-kid-out-of-college-trying-to-find-out-how-to-establish-a-living-before-they-shut-me-down-and-you-come-in-here-giving-me-a-hard-time-when-I've-got-work-to-do' look.

—I'm sorry, she said. She was not, though, he knew. She was only re-grouping. And, sure enough, after a short sip of the tea, she asked — How did the vote go in your district last night?

—What vote?

—The primary.

—What primary?

He watched her put on her best incredulity. —You didn't *vote*? She said it with shock and horror.

—I've been off in deep space. I just got back in a body.

—There are absentee ballots.

—I was trying to juggle a million things.

—It's the most important election you will probably ever live through.

Don't you *care*?

He did care. He knew the issues, and he had planned to vote. But there was something about the way she lay down on the word *care*, stretched out and rolled around on it, that put his back up.

—Come off it, Tish.

That was a bad choice. Now she waved her arms and literally shouted at him. —Come *off* it? *Off* it? Are you saying you don't care one way or the other that millions of people are being slaughtered every day, right now, being killed, and you can just sit back and drink your tea and not *care*?

He tried a change of vocal tenor. He tried looking in her eyes. —I do care. You know I do.

But it was too late. She was off. —I don't think you really do. The people of the universe have a chance to turn out the most bloodthirsty and repressive regime in the history of mankind, and you don't even bother to take the time to push one button. It's really that great a bother? You can't find *ten seconds* to try to save millions of lives, to give people just a shot at being free?

—Tish, I'll try to vote in the general.

—You just don't really *get* it, she said. You're off probably dreaming about the Dark.

Which showed exactly how out of it she was, for even the middlebrow magazine writers had finally caught on that people called the Fire the Fire now, not the Dark. But, to be fair, it also showed how perceptive she was, on some animal level, for in fact, as soon as she started talking about politics, he had drifted off thinking about the Fire.

> *Nothing is long enough –*
> *time isn't*
> Robert Creeley
> "The Tunnel"

T.J. looked up an old friend who was a resident at a hospital in Brooklyn Heights. Swallow drove out there with him, to make sure he made it okay.

Lang hadn't been at the apartment—he'd been at Johanna's—but he was coming back tonight. Marla couldn't see Swallow for a week. While T.J. was talking to his old friend the resident, Swallow was on a pay phone calling up and down the East Coast looking for an out. He found Blue in North Carolina. There was a train that went right there. Swallow got T.J. to drop him at Grand Central, and he was walking up to Blue's place that night.

Gray had seen the Fire exactly once. Kip, going to school in Sutter, had been after Gray and Turk to come visit him for months. So finally they did, knocking Turk's decrepit beater across seventeen clusters to see him. It was a good visit, lying around Kip's place talking and being easy. They stayed two weeks, intending every night to get up the next morning and leave, but staying until they caused Kip to fail all his examinations. They finally only left because the Fire were playing in Greenswood Hole. The beater broke down on the way to Greenswood, so they missed the party promised by friends there, and they almost missed the show. A note at the friends' place, when they finally found it, said 'Tickets and highs and us waiting for you at portal 1016. Hurry, dammit.' They hurried, but it took some doing to find the theater, and then to get to the right portal. When they finally got to the gate, Nicole was looking very impatient. —I thought you weren't going to make it.

They followed her to a locker room, got rid of their skins, and then were ushered out into the empty space, where their places were saved. They weren't the best seats possible, but then, nowhere in a deep-space theater is bad. Bird was already out tuning up, random cracklings and streaks of sound, light, radiation in all spectra, a testing modulation of energy, matter, and the fabric of space and time. Gray had just barely settled in and got comfortable when all the other members of the Fire appeared. Background existence, light and sound, matter and energy, space and time, dimmed slowly and were gone, and he was alone in an endless, empty universe, alone even from himself, a conscious non-being, in an endless nowhere Nothing.

A light came out of the east. A whirling came out of nowhere. And music came out of every cell of the Nothing. And then life was rolling out everywhere before him, endless, undulating. Thunder like a breaking open of the spheres, and a roar beyond the thunder like a new day coming on the flood. Then the thunder was a rhythm, and the roar became a song, and the Fire were into their first arrangement.

After that, Gray would have difficulty saying what happened, because there was no him there to record it. The Fire played directly upon him, modulating his self, making it as much a part of the arrangement as was the fabric of space and time. It was all breathing and glowing, with occasional thunder. Gray remembered later that he saw the birth and death of galaxies, heard music that had existed before man, experienced the feelings of volcanic rock and of stars going nova, knew colors inside no colors, found, for the first time ever, the universe a whole and himself a whole and the two of them each containing the whole of the other, both of them ebbing and advancing, rolling and screaming, riding across the emptiness. Space expanded until electrons whined, ricocheting across the night, and, in time, in another part of the tune, matter drew in on itself until all existence everywhere was a small glowing pink ball in the distance. In a descant, time was thickened into jelly, then into a solid, snapped into hard pieces and set bouncing in a dance rhythm. The distance shuddered and was pale. Gray later remembered a point in the arrangement when the rolling thunder drew back and a sweet, clear trickling ran across space, and he found himself swallowing the burning, bitter Time, feeling it glow within him, all through him, all Time. He remembered lashing and groaning, and an ominous changing far under the fabric of consciousness. And he remembered all his life, and all he had ever believed, and been, spread out before him, true and real and present again, laid out before him plain as day, spread out like a banquet. Then it was picked up again and the flow took it in, and he saw it turned, and twisted, and modulated, in and out of phase, growing and metamorphosing, straining the limits of existences, the walls of eternity shimmering and shaking, and then a rush as of waters or death, and it was all laid out simple again before him, only new from having been made different, simple, pure and sweet again now, presented before him, and Bird was humping it to beat holy hell, driving it, picking it up and shaking it, wringing every drop of intensity out of it.

It built that far and then became intermittent. The Everything-intensity, black-Nothing pause, the Everything again, lashing again, again, again, again . . . held for one long forever, then Nothing.

Wake up to existence in the still empty blackness of Greenswood Theater.

The Fire had finished their first number. The blackness tingled in aftershock. Gray felt numb, and very old. A hole opened then in the blackness, and an infinite choir of trumpets sounded. Gray felt himself pulled into the hole in the blackness and through it to the new space on the other side.

There were forever many more, one after the other, with only the brief, tingling pause in blackness between them. It went on long beyond the time when it seemed to Gray that all the life he had ever had before the Fire was no more than a poor introduction, a cheap, bad recording put on to entertain spectators while the Fire tuned up. Then one time out of the empty black tingling, instead of another new existence, came the quiet background matter of the theater. Gray and Turk and four million other human souls left very quietly, went out and put their tiny bodies back on, got into their transportation and took off for home.

Gray and Turk drove straight through, not stopping except for once to fix a motor, neither of them sleeping, the entire way home, raw from what they had seen, and felt, and been, raw, new-born, tingling, the two of them sitting inside the clear plastic of the beater, surrounded by night and true space, raw from visions and new truth.

I will tell you what meeting her is like. You will come, eventually, to a place and time when the liberation and surrender of accepting one more is neither so attractive nor so damned necessary as is the liberation and surrender of leaving, and going home, alone, to your own bed, to lie in darkness, dehydrate, roll, and sleep. You stand. You discover man was never intended to stand. He was designed for mud, not to sway like trees and gods. Having discovered that, you discover you are standing. Then, in that clear uncomplicated rare coherent consciousness which really does exist there, no matter how absolutely everyone, even yourself, ridicules twisted, stumbling ones, you manage to convince your host and his entire party that they have discovered or created the ultimate sweet perfect flow of communion, and your departure only means you can't keep up, that's all, and you're going away appreciative of the rich fine taste with which you've been honored, hoping to be invited back for more, soon, as soon as you recover. And then you are alone, in your slightly chilly and more than slightly complex vehicle. You manage, as you always somehow manage, to engineer it into motion, and then, very soon, much sooner than you had thought possible, or prudent, you are alone on a hollow of headlight and highway, alone with your terrible muddled lucidity, a still-growing undexterity and an ever-increasing forward speed.

It is a long drive home, an unlit two-lane mountain road. The road is almost always empty, and it is very late now, all god-fearing men home with their families' muffled snoring and their mortgaged rafters' creaking —the road is like virgin desert. At first you are slow and over-cautious in your hollow of headlights, to compensate for motor-skill impairment, lazy slow like a Sunday drive was always supposed to be. But every highway has a pull, and it is an irresistible pull at night, in the hollow, alone. Soon you feel the curves in your upper arms, soon you're drifting a little as you power out of them, heels and toes clicking pedals to feed road to motor and motor to road, and the rising and falling of motor and road meld into flows like tides would be if you were moon-cold feeling them tug and resist and subside in a cycle you knew in your bones and craters, the cornering audible now, but smooth and flowing still, and still the highway pulling, and it pulls you into your favorite tight blind narrow-bridge climbing corner, and you hit it hard, finding the right line through it for the first time in hundreds of tries, acing that corner, feeling—and exploiting—for the first time its full potential. And then she is there. Explosive, sudden glare in your lane, oncoming, and close.

The numb urgency is fast as the explosion of glare. It is a measure of the speed of consciousness, though, how long the mindfear lags behind the instantaneous bodyfear. It is a long time before that second wave breaks over you, in surges the awareness that only the twisted and crazed ever wander up this canyon, and only the most twisted and most crazed would be hauling down out of it at this time of night. In crests the awareness that the consciousness screaming into the curve at you this instant is at this instant as bent and as frail as yours is. And then spreading like ripples in the flood's still hollow the awareness of just how bent and frail yours is.

> *We could become superheroes or Nothing.*
> Ken Kesey, quoted in
> *The Electric Kool-Aid Acid Test*

He stopped at the gate, looked around for the dog. The house sat a quarter-mile back, on a light hill. Smoke rose from the chimney. He could see no dog.

He let himself through the gate. There was still no dog when he stepped onto the raised porch. A person in a jean shirt answered his knock.

—Is Steven here?

He hadn't known how to ask after Blue, but she turned and called — Blue! —then motioned him in.

Her name was Sarah. He was too wasted to do more than summarize his whole life for the two of them for about an hour and demand a horizontal area.

—You can try this couch if you want to, said Sarah with an armful of blankets, but I recommend the floor in Blue's study. You want a shower?

—In the morning.

On the floor in the study he found a bearskin in front of a fire. He dreamed of gulls in great winds, and kindling snapping in a dry frost.

Sarah found him in the kitchen in the morning with her recipe files.

—Is it okay? If you've secrets you'd rather not share . . .

—I've only a few, and none involve food.

—I like your proportional notation system.

—I don't know. My whole life has been like that. Incredibly involved private systems for things there are perfectly good systems for you can get for free.

—These didn't come out of books.

—When I was fourteen and fifteen, those two summers, I used to play all day in the kitchen. I hadn't any friends. Too heavy. Too smart. Too acne. Mom worked. Dad was in Newport Beach with his blonde chippie secretary floozy whore. I cooked all day. Crank up the stereo, Dad left his stereo, McIntosh power amp, guys always like it when I tell them that. Crank up 'Back in the U.S.S.R' till it shook the patio doors, and throw food around the kitchen. Mom was an appreciative audience. She never cooked that much herself, but if I asked her she could show me how. I never ate anything, I lived on diet pills, but it was like I finally found something I could do and it was so much fun. All the textures, all the kinds of smells. And now there's never any time. I wonder, like, after you grow up, do you just never get that back? Do you just have to go through a stretch when you're our age of having no time, or do you just never get it again?

They cooked a breakfast together, quick and light but self-congratulatory: shirred eggs, croissants with blackberry jam, and grapefruit sherbet. She made sherbet for breakfast, rapidly and without fuss. Blue struggled wet-haired and incoherent into the kitchen just in time to consume it and kiss her goodbye.

—I'll be late tonight. Don't wait dinner, I'll probably eat in town. I might stay over and save the drive. If I do, I'll call you. Dal, tell him these things some time after noon, and I won't bother to write them on the fridge.

—And you, Jelly was saying, do you ever even think of how much power you're wasting?

Gray looked up at her.

—I mean, you're not an ignorant person. You read. Doesn't it ever get to you that there are people freezing to death while you fiddle with your toys?

—I don't think of my tools as toys, Jelly.

—Well you should think about it. You know what the energy shortage is about. And still you go on playing with your expensive stuff. Don't you know that the energy you burn up to make pretty colors is energy that could be keeping people *alive*? Down in Attica, a whole colony could be given food and warmth for a year with the power you spend in a single day here. You *know* that.

He sighed. —Okay, Tish. What do you want? Another contribution to the Fund for the People? I could write you a bad check if it would make you happy.

—That's not the *point*. You know I'm right, and you know I know you know it. I've spent nights here when you didn't even turn off the sky when we went to bed. Left it all on, shining and spinning, and us inside a dark room with no windows. All night. And you've been to engineering school, you could probably write me all the equations to tell me exactly how much helium has to fuse to light up half a planet like a Roman candle all night when there's no one even watching it.

—Okay, Tish. I'll be sure to remember to shut it off when I turn in tonight.

He did not add, *alone*, although that was becoming clear.

—That's not the *point*. It's just your whole lifestyle, and all the *horrible waste*. We're using up three-quarters of the universe's resources, though we're less than one percent of one percent of the population. I bet you even keep the other side of this giant planet at full heat all the time, just so you won't have nasty old winds blowing in your face when you step outside. Huh? Am I right?

He did not answer. He wondered where Old Cat could have gone off to.

—So I'm sitting here wondering. I believe we all have conscience inside us, a small, still voice, and I'm sitting here wondering where yours is, what it's doing, or what you do with yourself so you don't hear it. I mean really. If you can't even think of the trillions of underprivileged people in the universe, some of them crowded ten thousand to a planet, think of *yourself*. What are you going to do when all the power is *gone*? When you wake up one morning very cold, and you turn up the heat, but nothing happens, because there's no power, none left anywhere, because it's all been wasted by people like you, playing with their pretty colors, and it's every bit of it gone, and you'll sit here in the dark getting colder and colder and then when the heat of your atmosphere radiates away and this planet starts heading down to absolute zero, what are you going to do then, Steven? What are you going to do then?

—Well, hon, I guess I'll put on my good Sunday dark suit and start practicing prayers.

—Steven, I'm being *serious*. You think there are an infinite number of stars for the power companies to strip? Next time you head across space to one of your parties, next time you burn enough power to last most civilizations a thousand years just to get to one of your Dark concerts, look around out there. It's getting pretty black out there. They're going. You look at the rate of them going, and you can see it's not much longer before they're *gone*. All that's left is the little galaxies down by San Pedro. And when they're gone, love, that's *all*. There aren't any more where those came from. So tell me what do you plan to do when you've used up everything there is to use up?

Gray poured himself another cup of tea. —I am really not as insensitive as you think. I didn't make the universe, and I really didn't single-handedly burn it all up to toast my bread for breakfast this morning, whatever you think of me, and I don't run the government and there's not a whole hell of a lot I could do about it if I wanted to, really, now, is there? If I shut down everything here and sat around waiting to freeze to death, so I'd never have to use an erg of power again, what difference would it make in the scope of the universe? Really? The army uses more power in every half-second of every one of its billions of bombing runs than I could use in a lifetime if I wanted to and if I could buy all the equipment there is and left it on full all the time. And, Tish, let me tell you, no matter what you think about your precious election, nobody has ever told an army what they can and cannot do.

She started to answer, but he cut her off. —Tish, I've got two or three centuries to go, and I'd like to make the most of them. I think the quality in man which produces art is the most important aspect of humanity we have. We have to hold onto that. If we throw that away, we're throwing away the whole point.

She started again, and he cut her off again. —So if you are through with the lecture on my lowdown ways, I was trying to get these sketches in at least some sort of reasonable shape for the people for Inca, so I won't spend the last few centuries of the human race in prison for fraud, embezzlement, accepting money under false pretences, and non-payment of debts, if it's okay by you.

Jelly Cornfish looked down at the table, and her delicate eyelashes quivered. —Okay, Steven, she said. I'm sorry.

He knew she was not sorry. She was only re-grouping.

> *For some the ransom came. For some there was Nothing.*
> Joanne Greenburg
> *The King's Persons*

They walked the farm after Swallow showered. Blue and Sarah owned a couple hundred acres of pine bottomland. A creek crossed from east to west, a railroad from north to south.

—I haven't been able to listen to freights at night since we lived up Coal Creek.

—Those were good trains, that one just an hour before dawn.

Blue kicked a trestle. —Look at this shit, all rotted out. Trains can't run more'n ten, fifteen miles an hour through here.

—That's disgusting.

—You ought to see the track under weight. One rail'll sink a foot lower'n the other, you expect the train to roll right over.

—A system that can't even run its trains, how you expect it to handle plot, character, diction, thought, spectacle or song? Like how hard is it to put down two sticks of steel and keep them down?

—It ain't for lack of knowing how. They had better roads through here in the 1840's.

—Your cattle?

—No. We lease the rights. He gives us three beef a year to boot. Same with the cropland. One reason we eat so good.

They returned to the house, approaching it from the rear.

—My lab.

It was an addition, slatted maple like the house.

—House was built in 1840. We put up the addition last summer, me'n Sarah.

Swallow stood in the hall between the living room and the addition, looking at the odd joints, out of square, molding four inches wide at top, half an inch at bottom.

—I built my part true to the world. The old house leans against itself. I thought about building true to the old house. I guess it would've looked better, would've been true to the eye. But I figured, my part will outlast the old, and there's no sense passing error on. Anyway, I like it better, I feel better inside it.

There was equipment Swallow didn't recognize. He studied what looked like a spectroscope only made of huge magnets, trying to figure out its read-outs. Blue's last lab had had dials and gauges. Now it was all digital LED's. Is it silly to be sentimental about gauges? Swallow had liked the white faces and the crisp black enamel ticks.

—Here, you can help me pull a crystal.

Blue kicked the black lights on, unstoppered a bottle, fixed the crystal in silver forceps wrapped in cheesecloth.

Five minutes later they had the crystal under an electron microscope. Blue took Polaroids. Swallow studied them as they came out of photographic chaos, but he recognized nothing on them.

—What you got here?

—I don't know yet.

—Got any ideas?

—A couple.

—Now we vat it?

—Ain't got no vats.

Swallow looked around. He could see no vats.

—What are you up to, Blue?

—Let's sit down over some tomato juice and talk.

Blue sealed the crystal, filed the photos, and over peppermint tea— there was no tomato juice in the cellar—he explained to Swallow how he'd gone over to pure research.

—Finally made enough to retire?

—Six years in the business, I was exactly even. Then the Amherst bust cost me sixty-five grand.

—Lawyers.

—Thank god for 'em, man. Sixty-five grand beats ten to twenty. Thank god for Sarah.

—She popped for sixty-five grand?

—She *borrowed* it.

—Jesus. Where?

—On her paper. She had a newspaper, in Amherst.

Swallow looked at the floor a while, thinking about the women he'd known.

—How in Christ's name did you pay her back?

—Never did.

Swallow poured some more tea. They sat, silent a while.

—She lost the paper. Bank took it. Good paper, too.

—So where'd all these acres in North Carolina come from?

—Sarah got another paper.

—Rich parents?

—Built it out of nothing, out of the back of a station wagon. She's good, Cooch. Dropped out of high school, ran away, worked on an underground rag, never went back. Bank down here trusts her for about a half a million American, and she's got some real estate folks own part of the business, but she's got control. We're clear in four years. Own the farm outright in four more years. Dig it, we live on a dollar a day.

—A dollar a day.

—Food's free. Power comes off a windmill. I sew our clothes. The dollar is for luxuries.

—And the lab?

—Sarah set me up, before we bought pots and pans, before we had curtains, before she had clothes. 'I've seen men lose their work,' she said. We've got a lot of respect for each other.

—You got that whole pretty lab, and you don't turn out ANYTHING?

—Oh, sometimes, a quiet night, Sarah and me'll pull out a taste. The sounds here. Not like the mountains, or New England, or the plains, or anywhere I ever been. Thicker. Some other kind of whole dimension on it. We got a rocker on the back porch we built, solid enough for us to sit two in it.

—You make all this stuff and just take PICTURES of it?

—What you want, Cooch? You want me to get sent up?

—So they beat you. They beat you, Blue, they beat you down.

—Here.

They went back into the lab. Blue pointed at a wall. It was all bookshelf. There were a few books, but most of the wall was covered with uniform black notebooks two inches thick.

—Pick one.

Swallow pulled one out of the center and leafed through it. Then he pulled another down. Six or seven more. He sat down with one, for a long time, then put them all back and started going down the wall reading only the covers.

—Oh, he said when he finished.

—Yeah. But dig it. Blue lifted from his desk a hand-bound leather volume. —My theoretical work.

When Swallow looked up a long time later Blue was still standing at parade rest before him.

—Okay, bud. I was talking out of my asshole.

—Lucky it's the first time that ever happened.

—Let me look at you awhile. I want to tell my great grandchildren about you.

—Let's go have a tomato juice on it.

When there is the Fire, and you and the Fire are there together, one existential working unit, so the creation of the Fire by human beings and your own act of creation in perceiving the Fire and that action-thing which is the nature of the Fire itself are all one and the same great thing, it is as though that union was always and always shall be. But then the Fire is over and gone and past and it becomes the time of after the Fire.

Which is probably as it should be. If you came all the way across the universe to know the Fire, and if you were of the Fire and it of you as the Fire reached ultimate intensity and reached beyond the Nothing, and if the Fire never ended, or if you died at the end of the last arrangement of the Fire, the Fire would have done nothing for you, and you would die as much a child as ever, for the time of the Fire is not your own time, it is the Fire's time and you were only there with it, and your time is the time beyond, when even the Fire and its ultimate visions are only one thing of the many things which exist in a life that is yours only.

And you leave the Fire and go home, wherever you came from to be with the Fire. You have been with the Fire and now you are alone apart from it except as its memory is within you still, and you go back to where you were before the Fire ever was. Even that world now seems not the world you left, but that world passed through the Fire; you see the world and remember the world the way you saw it before the Fire, but now that way is only one worn way of seeing, and does not include in it all you saw in the Fire; and this is your time now, time for making your own world real again after seeing beyond its ends in the Fire; this is your time.

Gray saw the Fire in Greenswood Hole, and then the Fire was over and gone, and Gray and Turk came out of the deep-space theater and got into the old beater and went home. And Gray said goodbye to Turk at Turk's place, no thanks, he didn't think he should come in and have breakfast. And then Gray went alone to his own home. And his own home was there. The knotty sap-dripping pine kitchen table was there. The cold rock of the valleys falling down away from his cabin had not moved. His rivers ran forever away, looking silver and unmoving in the distance. In his sky the quiet, luminescent moon he had left on still diffused in mist. There was tea. There was Old Cat. It was all there.

But Gray was not there as he had been before. He had always before been there as a man who had always before been there, who had always lived on worlds, if not this one then one like it. Now he was on the world as one who had been outside all worlds, who had seen the depths of space, who had seen galaxies like swarms of bees melt into flowing honey, who had seen the birth and death of all being, who had seen beyond the wall where matter curves in on itself, who had walked in light and bathed in darkness, who had seen the machinery of everything everywhere disassembled before him and laid out on a table, bronze gears gleaming, who had seen the parts re-wired into a giant steam calliope on which men, human beings, creatures of which he was one, played out their visions.

He had seen these things, and now he stood again on one small world, rock floating in a loose cluster in one small pocket off to the edge of things; he stood there, on his world; and he felt no longer a creature of worlds, but a creature of deep space and a being beyond even the deepest space, beyond all places, a creature of out-there. He was an out-there being now, who only just happened at the moment to be living within a conventional world structure.

After just one time at the Fire, Gray believed he belonged there all the time. Actually, it would not probably have taken even as much exposure as he received. Even the most fleeting vision beyond the world is enough. Just to know that the world you have known is not all there is. If man is anything worth being, all he has to do is to see, one time, that there is more, and he will declare him a citizen of what lies beyond.

> *Nothing*
> *Remembered who I was*
> W.S. Merwin
> 'The Recognition'

There was a greenhouse. The tomatoes looked green to Swallow, but Blue found a few that he approved. In the kitchen, drinking the juice, they talked about it.

—I came to the point where I didn't believe in it any more. The potential was real enough, but just nothing around for it to work on. Like, you drop a perfect crystal into a kettle of piss, all you get is a kettle of piss. Same old kettle, same old piss.

He could be apart from Blue for months at a time, in this case years, yet when they locked back up it turned out they'd been all the same places.

—I might as well have been running a pickle factory, Blue went on. You turn a product over to distributors and the bland-faced consumers take it.

Swallow nodded. —Doesn't matter what you put in it if they don't know it's there. Hey, you seen the androids?

—What androids?

—They have seams in their necks. They're androids. Somebody is manufacturing them and sticking them where people used to be.

—I ain't seen no androids. Who needs 'em? The people they got are just as good as androids. You sure you saw androids? How could you tell the difference? They could all be androids for all I could tell. Put god on a blotter and they just keep on rubbing that thing.

—So you quit.

—Yeah, but you can't quit. Sarah's right. So I started thinking about what nobody was working on learning. We're all gonna take a big step out some day. Might be a thousand years, or it might be tomorrow, but we *are* gonna take that step. And when we get ready we gonna need to *know* some things.

—You got copies of this?

—Yeah, in real safe places.

—Steven, she said, we need to talk about us.

What he thought then was—God, let's go back to politics gain. Tell me again what a cruel elitist I am, lecture me on the state of the universe, anything, please, but please, please, let's not get started on that. Please?

What he said was—I'm really exhausted, Tish. Can we talk about it in the morning?

—I think we need to talk about it now, she said.

He sat very still, and only realized after quite some time that he had stopped breathing.

But I have been negligent. We've been talking of Swallow this whole time, and I don't believe I have told you anything about what he looks like. Everyone said he was skinny. He thought of himself as skinny. It is true that his shoulders were narrow and his bones thin. His forearms were still skinny. His face was almost round. Only a closely cut beard, where a chin would have been if he had any chin—he did not—kept the face from rounding like Charley Brown's. His chest was sunken, you could count his ribs, but his middle was starting to bulge. There was some loose flesh drooping over what had once been bony hips.

His forehead had always been high. It probably looked no different now than it did in his high school graduation picture—an expanse as high as your hand is wide, curved back, lined only faintly, almost always tanned, even in winter. The hair was parted—it had always been parted—on the left, high, crookedly. On that side, it hung down about the length and shape, though not the color, of a surfer's in 1965. On a bad day it went down to an inch above the ear and then stuck straight out like Bozo's. The rest of the hair was combed right. Sometimes it looked light and wavy, sometimes windblown like an early Dylan, sometimes Bozo on that side too. I never once saw it look like it was cared for, never as though he had just combed it, or just had it cut. It always looked like he'd been out working under the car. The color was that color hair you can't call any color, like leather colored only by sweat.

His nose was thin, straight, narrow and long, ending too high up in his forehead, not down between the eyes where a nose ought to end. He always wore glasses, though, so you couldn't tell that it ended too high. Down at the other end it was still growing longer. After the bone ended, the nose continued to grow. Now there was a pointy, droopy piece of flesh that hadn't been there when he was a child. It was changing the straight line into a slight downward arc.

His chin bones were present enough to create a face, but not so present as to call attention to themselves. His left ear had a mole where the hole for an earring would be—just the size of a turquoise-stud earring. In fact, it was sometimes mistaken for an earring, as the earpiece of his glasses hung down too long and showed silver below it. The glasses were plain, round wire-frames, the kind everyone had worn back in 1969. He had bought the glasses in 1969 and worn them every day since.

His posture had once been terrible and was now merely bad. His weight settled onto an axis—before it had fallen over one way or another. He did have that way of standing, but unless you were talking to him for a while, and something clicked, and he got interested in something either you or he was saying, you'd never see him rise up on the balls of his feet like that. There was that grin, but he handed that out real selectively. What you might observe, if he were sunk in thought, is his hands on his face, crawling like spiders, fingers twisting and twining across his lips, up his cheeks, scratching his head, tugging his ears. But even that, depending on the day, you could also follow him all day and not ever see him enter that almost fugal state.

You know how neighbors say about serial murderers, after their crimes are exposed, 'I never really noticed him.' If Swallow walked into your establishment, you wouldn't look at him twice, and you'd have nothing helpful to tell the police when they came later to inquire. After a party, if you tried to describe him to someone who didn't know him, they wouldn't remember they had seen him. — Are you sure he was there?

> *Nothing can stop the United States of America.*
> Gerald Ford
> 9:37 EDT 12 August 1974

Sarah called to say she wasn't coming home that night, then T.J. called to say he was. In fact, he was just down the road, not even lost but merely out of confidence, about two miles short on faith. He still wasn't eating, but he could sit upright and talk. Blue and Swallow entertained him with stories of old times: the riots on the Hill, Swallow's polka band, the time Blue rolled a borrowed Ferrari off Flagstaff, the time the coal-fired water heater blew in Telluride. Derek Whitmore.

—How'd you never hear about him? Cooch, you got so many stories now you don't tell your friends about your brush with fame and death? Derek was chairman of College Republicans and Campus Crusade for Christ. We used to do nitrous together, when Hal drove the truck for Dental Supply.

—Derek got his Jesus from Kierkegaard and his politics from William O. Douglas. Only man in Colorado you could talk to about Boethius and Augustine.

—I never thought he knew assways from Sunday about Augustine. Knew his Capellanus by heart, though.

Both laughed.

T.J. was irked. They had been showing off. They had been in-joking.
— So is there a story?

Blue returned to peeling avocados. Swallow looked at T.J., thinking of T.J. laughing nervously at parties, of the barely perceptible whitening of T.J.'s knuckles every time Swallow drove the long outside curve in Boulder Canyon.

—Derek got offed one night in Boulder. Coming out of Shannon's bar.

—Pigs thought it was me, Blue said.

Swallow began thinking of the white water in the shallow creek, the night he and T.J. pulled the high school couple out, the long wait for the ambulance, the chill of the water, the stench of burnt foam rubber, the unacceptability of twisted flesh, the implacable circulation of the red lights when they came, their even sweep on the irregular canyon wall.

Blue stopped peeling avocados. —Cooch and me stopped in for a beer. Used to go out ever Thursday night, after quant. Somehow the DEA was lookin for me. Lookin for Cooch here, too. I think they thought you was my accomplice instead of just a sycophantic hanger-on. They saw Derek go in with us. When we come out he was walking ahead. They yelled to flatten up against the wall. Derek, he fucked up.

—Jesus, man, he was a fucking Republican. What do Republicans know about cops on the street?

—He tried to put away the pack of mints he was holding, before he put his hands up.

—To get the beer smell off his breath, before he went home.

—He tried to put them in his jacket pocket.

Blue looked down at the green film on his hands. —Ever' once in awhile I think of that rhythm. Boomboomboom . . . boom . . . boom.

—The way his body took the slugs. Slamslamslam . . . slam . . . slam.

—Like when you hit a frog with juice, how he came up off the sidewalk for number five.

T.J. nodded. —Like '70?

—Yeah. Why?

—Five hundred eighty-seven police murders in 1970. The year they cracked down. Tapered off to three hundred sixty-two in '71, been holding steady since in the low three hundreds.

—Jesus, Cooch, where you get this guy? He never had a friend before? What man, all you got is numbers, you've never met any people?

T.J. cringed. — Blue, I'm sorry. I do it all the time. That's why Linda left me. One reason, anyway. Did I tell you, Dal, about the last night on Oak Street? I woke up, it was about three o'clock in the morning, I woke up and Linda is sitting on the chair by my bed with the butcher knife from the kitchen. 'Linda, how long have you been sitting there, Linda?' 'I have been sitting here since ten o'clock, Thomas.' 'Linda, come to bed, Linda.' 'Thomas, if you find yourself alive in the morning I want you to take me back to Richmond. I want the savings account because it's mine, I earned it. It's my money. And I want the rugs and my Aunt Margaret's china.' 'Linda, things look different in daylight. Come to bed Linda.' 'Not any more, Thomas. Not any more.' She really hated the numbers, man. I'd come out with a number and she'd, like, well— anyway, sorry. How'd it come out?

—Justifiable homicide. Of course. Didn't get past the coroner's inquest.

—No, of course, I mean, with you two.

—Charged with like, what was it, Cooch, obstructing justice?

—Interfering with police procedures?

—Shit, and I thought the verbal facility was supposed to be the last to go. I thought I'd never forget the wording. Impeding an officer of the law?

—Anyway, the D.A. deferred prosecution and suggested a change of address. Blue, how you and the law get along these days?

—Pretty good. D.A. hereabouts is a friend of Sarah's, his wife is her photographer. He likes my record collection.

—He know about your shady past?

—How'm I gonna hide it? I got a year of probation to go.

—And?

—It's all cool. He's taken the tour of my lab.

—Lord, things that degenerate here?

—No, man, it's all straight. I promise to do nothing illegal, he promises to squelch any local attempts to harass me.

—Blue, I read your journals.

—Cooch, *think*. *Think*, Cooch. That stuff ain't illegal. I've never told anybody about it. How can they pass a law against what they never heard of?

For a minute Swallow was a legislator trying to outlaw Blue's work proactively, and then he was deep in the tense structure of English trying to make it all work. Eventually he got so tangled he gave it up. —So is that why you don't have a dog?

—Huh?

—I noticed you don't have a dog. Is that why?

— Uh, no. I ain't had a dog since Oak Creek. Novalis, you remember that Shepmoyed? Tore up a kid one day, walking home from school. Had to shoot her.

—Like, with a gun?

—I used to keep a gun. A paranoia pistol. Smith and Wesson. Put two thirty-eight slugs in her head and buried her under the tomato patch. Best dog I ever had.

— So what'd you do with the pistol? You want to teach me how to tear up tin cans?

—Huh-uh. I melted it down. Didn't want to own no gun I'd used to shoot my own dog. It's that ugly green ashtray in the front room.

His father dies (that is what the bell is ringing to say) and is buried, leaving him in the care of his grandmother the witch. His grandmother's mind is tangled like old snarls of wire, and when she gets him alone he feels his tender consciousness is at risk of flickering out. He spends as much time as possible at school. There is a new girl at school, from the capital. Diane. He is desperate with loneliness and desire. Diane is cool as willow branches. She does not believe in the gods. She sees wider than he does, and through she does not mock him or openly laugh, she cannot help communicating her amusement at his perpetual naiveté and clumsiness. Diane teaches him culture, manners, politics, books, and hopes. He wants to possess her. She wants to go to the capital. They run away together, him fearful at every turn. In the capital her knowingness finds a place for them to stay and friends. He in his fear and unknowledge is paralyzed and furious. She never gives herself to him. Police come. She goes back to the provincial village. Swallow is left in the capital alone.

The Lothis, giving audience and dispensing justice in the square, asks a rhetorical question. Swallow answers. The Lothis tells guards to bring him along to the palace. There he is dressed in white silk and allowed to sit at the Lothis' feet during private audiences. The Lothis asks him for his view and follows it. The Lothis' concubine is black-haired and bejeweled. Whenever the Lothis is away, she brings the boy to her and he struggles to satisfy her lusts. She plays with him like a cat. The Kaalds are uniting to depose the Lothis. The Lothis develops a siege mentality. The boy has become a source of ridicule. The Lothis begins neglecting him. A session of the Kaaldic is set. The boy makes a plan to conspire with the Kaalds. The Lothis discovers Swallow's relations with his concubine and banishes him, orders him far away to school. En route, he hears that the Lothis has fallen.

At the academy he studies the ancients, history, alchemy, philosophy.

She is a music student. He knows he does not love her because he is not yet king. She does not need for him to say he loves her. But he needs that. He needs to be in love. He grows to resent her not needing him the way he needs to need her; he grows to resent the lies which convince neither of them and which she doesn't even need as he needs. He studies with an unbalanced fire. She is grounded in her art. His art warps and shivers him. He decides to commit himself to her, though she says she does not need for him to do so. When he cannot, he cuts himself off from her and lives alone.

Alone in the mountains, he fasts during long vigils. He keeps notebooks. His need for power is like a river in flood. The need for people is like a desert in him. He flagellates himself. He attends a necrophilic black ritual, which is where he meets her. She eats the flesh of the unborn. She has shuddering nightmares. She has been hurt, and hurt again, and then hurt more. She parches for love. He slides through her armor and they marry. They move to the capital where she has a job. She wants him to get a job. Devoted to her, he tries, and repeatedly fails at every profession he assays. He tells her, gradually, of his visions. She opposes them. She shows them for the disease they are. Every boy has that vision. It is time for you to become a man now, and give up those boyish dreams. They have a daughter. He becomes sick. He vomits blood. He is dizzy. Stars swirl around him. He becomes assistant to a Kaald. The hours are long and keep him from her. She knows what current draws him away. He loses his love for her. They become enemies locked together. He becomes a Kaald. Doors open easily for him. Skills he has no ability to wield at home come fluidly to him in the centers of power. When he manipulates his way to become Lothis, she erupts in a torrent of fear and anger. They move to the palace and are never the same together. He uses his stature to distance himself from her. When it is clear he is determined to become king, she leaves him.

He turns to a white-haired young virgin from the country whom he pampers and depraves. By the time she turns on him, he is king, and he has her executed. His plans all turn back on him. He is convinced by his own experience that the only human motives are base ones. His best endeavors are the most resented. He begins to use power for self-indulgence. He becomes malicious. He enjoys punishing his enemies. His appetites become cruel. He becomes anhedonic and frenzied. He is deposed and serves years in prison.

Paroled, he retires to the seashore, tended by his daughter. Blind and sick, he finds a sort of peace, and wonders if the only true love is non-sexual, the love that is the binding of the species, the love that spans centuries. Still he burns with unknowing of himself. He composes songs that attempt to decipher the riddle. He floats back through the past, trying to incorporate it into a self. He can't figure out how to account for anything, but now he sees from others' eyes rather than his own.

He undertakes a pilgrimage to the gods—the gods he has lost, then mocked, then attempted to ban. He goes alone, sending his daughter into the care of a family where he hopes she will marry. He climbs the mountain. There he meets the magician. He descends inside the mountain. There he meets his true love, who was with him all the time. He does not die, but becomes young again, and whole, a farmer in the country, married and strong.

The phone rang. Jelly stopped talking. He looked in her silence, he studied the fine lines of her cheek and neck.

—Aren't you going to answer that?

—I really don't feel like talking.

—You don't even know who it is.

—I still don't feel like talking.

Besides, he did know who it was. It was Taylor at Inca, and Gray would rather talk to Jelly Cornfish about their relationship than talk to Taylor. Taylor would start off with easy conversation about what was in the news and what each of them had been doing, and a new kind of nut, berry, pigment, shower scent or psychotropic drug, and then somewhere near the third quarter of the talk as measured in time elapsed, the question, phrased with no particular emphasis, just another subject of conversation, like the new scent —How you coming on the work?

Taylor would not be satisfied with Gray's 'Well, it's coming along, I guess.' He would push. Still asking in the same tone a friend might use —You finished the specs on the secondary chromatics?

Jelly stood up dramatically. —Well I think that's just horrible. If you're not going to answer it, I will.

She probably thought it was another woman, Gray realized. She wanted to answer the phone and find another woman calling him.

It was Turk.

—I didn't interrupt anything, did I?

Turk's tone was jovial. Turk was always jovial. —Wouldn't want to break in just when you and Ms. Cornfish were . . .

—No, Gray interrupted. I was just sitting here listening to her tell me about the sad state of the universe and the inevitable consequences of my lowdown ways.

—Yeah, that. Well, you tell her give 'em hell for me, will you?

—I will surely do that.

—Listen. I didn't call just to chat. I just found out from my sister that the Fire are in Jessup day after tomorrow, and I called a guy I used to know that works on one of their equipment crews, and he said he can get me tickets. You want to go?

—Hey, really?

—Yeah, really.

—Sign me up, man. When do we leave?

—I figure if we leave your place in a couple of hours we can just make it.

—So why are we talking on the phone?

Jelly was at him the minute the phone switched itself off. —See? And you weren't even going to answer it.

—Turk is going to be here in ten minutes, and I have a million things to do. I think we should finish this up when I get back. Okay? I'll call you the minute I get back, I promise.

She left huffy and hurt. Gray did not want her to leave that way, he only wanted her to leave. He had almost mastered the skill of getting her to leave unruffled, but it was a practice that took much time and more care, and which even at that was only slightly less than halfway successful. It didn't actually much matter. She would be back. She fluffed away busy being hurt, but she always came back.

> *and just lay there looking up
> at Nothing*
> Lawrence Ferlinghetti,
> *A Coney Island of the Mind*, #8

T.J. was hot to leave for Boston the next afternoon. Swallow wanted to see Sarah again, but T.J. was hot to leave.

Blue took him aside before they left. —I got a favor to ask.

—Shit, Blue, I gave up years ago trying to settle my debts to you. Just tell me, man.

—This'll do it. You got good timing showing up here now. I was looking for someone to trust with my stuff. I got to go up.

—Up?

—It's, it's like, shit, sometimes I wish you knew the technical side so I could explain it. It's meta.

—Meta how? What kind of meta?

—I can't tell you what it's like till I go there. And if I go I might not be able to get back.

—So objectify for me. You mean, like your brain fries and I come visit you in the vegetable bin?

—No. I mean, like gone. What there is, is, there's another chemistry. And I think like I've figured out the other chemistry. It's like, this is a third-order chemistry here—he kicked a table— and I've figured out how to build the fourth. Only it's like insubstantial. I mean, I guess what you'd probably call it is like pure consciousness. I mean, I guess that's how I been thinking of it. Only it's not. I mean, it just looks pure from over here. It's just as complex as, I mean, it's got all kind of structures. I mean, I think. I can't tell. It's hard to experiment. I mean, you can't do it with things. You got to go there.

—Is there a fifth?

—God, I love you. I remember the first time I showed you a fighter kite, I remember, I handed you the strings, and you very first thing start flying it straight at the ground. No. At least, I don't think so. I think you're limited by the number of dimensions.

—You think there's just four dimensions?

—Shit, man, I'm just a chemist, man, I'm just a basement fucking chemist. I ain't making up new dimensions.

—No, man, you're just going meta-chemical, that's all. So what does it mean to, like 'go there'?

—How do you know till you go?

Well, of course. How do you know till you go?

—So you think you might not come back?

—How do you know till you go?

Well, of course. How do you know till you go?

—So what's the favor? You told me you got your notes archived safe already.

—Cooch, I said a *favor*.

—Come on, Blue.

—If I'm gone for a month I want to you to come look for me.

—What do you mean, gone?

—I'll just fucking disappear man. Sarah will have a note saying I'm trying an experiment and it might make me disappear.

—You're not even going to tell her?

—Man, I couldn't tell her this.

—You are *scum*. You turd, you are scum from a rat's ass, man.

—Yeah, she makes an impression, don't she? Yeah. Well, man, Sarah and me, we been together three years and I love her and, man, I know how I love her and you don't. And I know what we got and you don't. You're just outside guessing, only you think you understand cause you're so fucking perceptive, only all you did was cook breakfast with her one time in North Carolina, you never had a miscarriage with her, you never saw her when she forgets her medicine, you've never seen her in the night, she's never pounded on your chest with her fists, you've never cried in her arms, you don't know *shit*, you're the stupidest motherfucker that ever walked, you're insensitive, you're blind, you're shallow, and you don't understand. Sarah and me is Sarah and me, man, and you don't have to take care of it. You couldn't if you tried.

—So you disappear and she gets a note saying you're gone.

—Maybe. Maybe I just go there and come back. Maybe I can go there and stay there. I don't know.

—But if you go and don't come back?

—I want you to follow me.

—You mean, like, you want a posse? You want me to cover you? The griffins might have you pinned down and you need another sorcerer to counteract their spell?

—I don't want to be alone.

Swallow didn't reply.

—If I don't come back, I want you with me. I need you, man. Pioneers. I need someone to talk to. I'd go crazy alone. I need you to keep me straight.

—How about Sarah?

—Jesus, will you let go of Sarah? You baked *croissants* with Sarah. You're impressionable. Remember Nancy? Remember what you thought about Nancy? Remember *Diane*? Remember Cindy? Remember Jori? Remember Toni *Brown*? Jesus, man. You think so straight about everything else.

—I can't promise. It's too fucking weird. It's too fucking big.

—I don't want you to promise. Shit, I just want you to do it. Here.

He handed Swallow a pendant on a gold chain. The pendant was the color of an eggplant, the size of a pumpkin seed. —Break it open and whiff it.

—I can't promise, man.

—I don't need you to promise, man, I just need you to have the pendant.

—I'll come give it back next year and we'll laugh.

—*You'll* laugh, man, ain't you never noticed I never laugh?

Heberlein quiz (10 points)

1. Describe Swallow's mother.

2. When was Swallow born?

3. Where is T.J. from?

4. List at least three names by which Swallow is called, and for each name, say who calls him that.

5. Describe one article of clothing worn by one character in this book.

Extra credit (particularly for those who have read ahead): One point for each of Swallow's aunts you can name.

It was twenty hours to Jessup. Turk's beater had a tape system in it, so they lay back and watched arrangements play themselves out in the emptiness. Jelly was right, there were very few stars out that way.

Jessup Theater was bigger than Greenswood Hole, where Gray had first seen the Fire. A cluster of boats, bugs, buses, and bubble tents stretched out like the very long tail of a very big comet. People lined up in advance, hoping for better seats.

Turk did not head for the line but set his beater down on a support world two systems distant from the actual theater. — I haven't seen Kilroy in years. We were almost the same person in school. Damn, what we didn't go through together.

Security challenged them, but after checking Turk's story, cleared them to land. Kilroy was not waiting for them at the port, but a message was.

>   Turk —
>
>>   In case you haven't heard, the performance is put off a week. Technical difficulties. To say the least. I've got tiny quarters here you're welcome to use; I don't think I'll be sleeping until I get things put back together. Look me up in the mixer board section. Show them this if they want to see something. Sorry the situation doesn't allow better hospitality.
>>
>>   —K. Roy
>
>   P.S. I've got your tickets with me.
>
>   P.P.S. My quarters are in Section Seven of

Zimbalist's, which is the next world up from the one you're on, in case you want to stash your gear or relax or anything before you come looking for me.

They did stop in at Kilroy's lodgings, which were cramped and Spartan, obviously a temporary mobile environment, like a circus tent or a camping trailer. They showered, had a massage, ate, and left to find Kilroy.

They found him suspended from a relay projector, upside down and sideways, with his hands full of maintenance leads, checking circuit boards. Gray whistled. —That's more Inca boards than I have ever seen. And I've been in their factory.

Kilroy looked at him. —You know Inca?

—Yeah, Gray said. I'm working on a design for them right now. Or supposed to be. If I weren't here.

—You want a job?

> *Flame itself, by Nothing fed*
> E.A. Robinson
> 'The Man Against the Sky'

T.J.'s friend in Boston turned out to never want to see him again. They cruised on up to Maine, camped on the island of Mount Desert, and ate lobsters until it started raining. As they had no tent, they fled. T.J. had developed an intricate rap on the virtues of the exoskeleton.

Phone work found a college roommate of T.J.'s in New Hampshire. It was a co-op. There were goats. There was a man in the co-op who one-upped Blue and Sarah by living without any money at all. This was not completely by choice. He had protested the war by not paying income tax, been convicted, and the IRS had put a lien on any money he would ever receive. So he had constructed a life that did not involve money. He traded his time for the time of others. T.J. and Swallow spent a pleasant afternoon with him asking everything they could think of about how it worked. The next day, Swallow and T.J. helped him rafter a barn. T.J. had never helped construct a building, and was full of comments on the structure of trusses.

They'd been there a week when Swallow saw the seam on T.J.'s neck.

—T.J., you're an android.

He didn't think, he just blurted it out.

—Yeah, man. What made you figure it out?

—Have you always been an android, or when did it happen?

—Last year. Remember Jan? Jan was an android.

—How does it work?

—It's a secret. You're never supposed to let it out. If you tell, they take your body away and leave you in a jar.

—Yeah, but this is like me.

—And you already know. How'd you find out?

—How does it work?

—It's not like being an android. It's more like riding an android. Instead of your body, you've got an android. The android is better. It sees better, it feels better.

—How come you got sick in New York?

—Androids get sick. Just not often. Trowbridge is an android doctor. I'm scareder of getting sick now than I used to be, because it's so much more unknown.

—What you do run on? How are you powered?

—Same as you. I break down food in combustion cells. Hell, you watched me eat lobster.

—Can you taste?

—I got all five senses. Smell is sort of ragged. They haven't got smell worked out totally. There's a lot of acrid like background noise. With your birthbody, if you're in a room for ten minutes you stop smelling it. I keep smelling it.

—What do they do, do they come in the night and kidnap your body?

—They recruit you. If they want you they have an android talk to you.

—You like volunteer?

—You say yes.

—Why?

—One, you're immortal. Want to live forever, man?

—You can recruit me?

—No. Like I said, they'll put me in a jar.

—How do they pick people? What are they after?

—They say they aren't after anything.

—Like, is it an underground? Are they gearing up to take over the world? You have meetings?

—Always looking for Mephistopheles, huh? Maybe you're right. Maybe fifty years from now someone will show up on my door and demand my service in the revolution. I don't think so. I don't think it's like that.

—What do you think it's like?

—I think it's like somebody has a vision. A vision of what we could be. A vision of enhanced humans. A vision of mind less fettered by evolution. A vision of the future.

—Is it free?

—The body cost twenty-three grand. Hell, people spend that on cars. There's a maintenance fee. It's like fifty bucks a month.

—Why the secrecy?

—Don't be stupid. You've seen how the right reacts to birth control pills. What do you suppose they'd say if they knew?

—They probably couldn't stop it. They'd freak out, but they probably couldn't stop it.

—You got to remember, Alan, you and everyone you know are way off the end of the bell curve, out two standard deviations from the mean. You think McGovern is middle of the road.

—What if you got hit by a truck and they took you to an emergency room?

—If my pulse stops, the body vaporizes. Some truck driver has an encounter with the paranormal.

—Still, the odds. Sooner or later, it comes out, and then the backlash is insane. They hunt you down with pitchforks.

—We're keeping it small. It's not a proselytizing movement.

—How many of you are there?

—I don't know. I can't always tell an android. How do you tell?

—The seams. There's a seam on your neck.

—There's no seam on my neck.

They hunted up a hand mirror and stood in the bathroom.

—See? Like a little line where the grains don't quite match.

—I still can't see it.

—The light in here isn't good. I can barely see it in here.

—You can see it, though?

—You have to be right up close and looking. I saw it on the train to Chicago. I had to get off the train. I think they saw me see them.

—What, you think androids are chasing you across America? Like *Invasion of the Body Snatchers*?

It sounded silly when T.J. said it.

—It's just like, don't you know anybody who ever did cognitive enhancers?

—I used to do magnesium pemoline. Never saw much improvement in my memory.

—That was a long time ago. They got better stuff now. I just mean, it's just like, people who do illegal drugs aren't in a conspiracy to hunt down the straights. They just want not to be noticed. It's like that.

—What's it like? Are you smarter?

—I've still got my same brain. They're working on brains. And they want to do consciousness without brains. Like, can you see spinning at lightspeed through a network with all the world's knowledge just like, right there, so you could just always have it, you'd never have to read a book, you'd have them all already?

—I think I'd miss my body.

—The body is so stupid. If you turned in a body as a project in basic design, what would you get? C-? D+?

—The body is where you feel pleasure.

—No, man. The body is just what sends telegraphs to where you feel pleasure. That's what most people plunk down the twenty-three grand for. Like, suppose an unlimited supply of, like, what's pleasurable? Like cocaine? I don't care for it myself, but lots of people seem to. You could have that, all the time. What I like is like, when you're falling just about ninety-percent asleep, in the sun, and your limbs feel warm, and you feel like you can just about float? I keep myself just about like that just about all the time.

—Can you have sex?

—Yeah.

—What's it like?

—It's like sex. Only you have more control. If you want to take three hours, you take three hours.

—So sex with another android must be pretty controlled.

—Sex with another android is like total freedom to do what your love wants you to do instead of just what your body will let you. Sex with another android is like what you fantasize.

—Linda wasn't an android.

No. Linda was a wonderful, sensitive, caring woman whose body didn't want her to have sex at all.

—So is there like gay android sex?

—Jesus, Dal. I guess there are probably gay androids. There are android mystics and libertarian androids and mainstream corporate androids. I mean, I'm still me. I still have all my memories. In fact, I've got *more* memories, I've got a lot clearer path back to really early childhood. And the body has all the regular connections. You eat, you shit. You just don't get hungry unless you want to feel hungry, and everything tends to work.

—And it's just capitalism? There's some factory in New Jersey where they build them, and they sell them on the black market?

—That may be the best way to look at it.

—What if I wanted to get one?

—I'll ask. You want one?

—I haven't got twenty-three grand. And I know you. I think you'd deny what you lose. I think after you got the android, if there was stuff you missed, you'd pretend you didn't. Could you go back?

—No. They mess up your old one getting you out.

—Well, there it is.

—I wouldn't want to go back, man. You can't imagine.

—Maybe I should like wait till I'm seventy and in a wheel chair, and then trade in.

—Maybe by then they'll be able to do that, but now it's like they won't take anyone over twenty-five. By then your brain has started degrading. Your body wasn't built to make it to thirty. By then you're already crapped out.

—So it's not just capitalism. I mean, they could just go after rich old geezers.

—No. You know, Dal, there are lots of people with visions. You and I weren't the only ones who grew up reading science fiction. Humans are headed on out. We've only started the trip. This is just the next phase of the trip. I think we'll go cybernetic soon. I want to be on that voyage. I've put in for cybernetic. It makes me shiver to think of it.

—Does it? I mean, that's just it. That's exactly it. Does it make you shiver? I mean, I think with my body. My body knows more than I do. My body is smarter than me. If I try to ignore it . . .

—Your body is smarter than you, but my body is smarter than yours. You think of it that way, but it's not really, it's only that that's where your neurons think they're having the thoughts. They're really having the thoughts in your neurons. I've got all that, just more subtle and conscious control.

—They wouldn't really put you in a jar? They don't have like the android police.

—It's a way of speaking. They make you promise. I'd hate to fuck it up for all of us. And I think they put in some inhibitions.

—Jesus, you're living in a body with built-in cops?

—You're not?

After the show, after Gray had seen Turk off, with a million instructions for how to put his world into cold storage until he got back there, including repeated entreaties to look for Old Cat, while Gray and Kilroy were stowing gear, Gray got to meet the leader of the Fire.

Kilroy was upside down in the projectors and didn't see him enter, but Gray did. He stood up.

—I'm Steven Gray.

Sticking out a hand, Bird said —Hi, I'm Alan Swallow.

Gray thought that was just about the funniest, and definitely the most engaging thing he had ever heard. Probably one of the three most famous people in the universe. Maybe just after the President in any survey of most recognizable names or faces in the universe, maybe ahead. To stick out his hand like that and say, as if you didn't already know, 'Hi, I'm Alan Swallow.'

After he had told this story about a thousand times, over many years, and after he had seen Bird do the same thing to other people countless times, in fact, infallibly on meeting another human being, Gray started to wonder if it was merely manipulative. After he had stayed up all night up one more time to fix something that was really basically all right, just because Bird got him to admit that it wasn't really *all* all right, after Bird somehow led him to *volunteer* to do so, Gray wondered whether the way Bird was with people wasn't just a way to get people to do things for him. That 'Hi, I'm Alan Swallow,' stuff was just part of it.

Later still, after they had been working closely together for years, Gray decided it was way more than that. It was the way Bird thought people should be. So he was. How Bird thought people should be, he was. And that, Gray realized, was exactly why he loved Bird the way he did.

In every new town, Swallow stops in first at a branch library. Not the big library downtown with guards at the door and concertina on the roof. Not the house of pretensions out at the university. But a neighborhood library, converted from an old house, where you can tell which room used to be the kitchen, where the unisex restroom is the old bathroom, toilet paper on a roll, the sink made of porcelain. Swallow spends a long time taking books off the shelf and looking through them. Among the adult books, he likes the local non-fiction best. But of all the books, his favorites are the children's books.

He always asks the librarian about Abigail Rain. When Swallow was young, his whole family, including grandparents and two sets of aunts and uncles, went one Thanksgiving to a great aunt's. Aunt Dorothy's. While the women were in last-minute frenzy before the feast, while the men were watching sports on television and the other children playing healthy vigorous games outdoors, Swallow was allowed to pore through Aunt Dorothy's attic. There was an improvised closet full of old clothes, including Uncle Albert's uniforms from World War I. There were locked trunks. Some old lamps and board games. And books.

Uncle Albert's horticultural guides. Mostly cheaply printed farm extension brochures recommending fertilizer levels. But then also the most beautiful book Swallow ever saw: a leather-bound catalog of peaches. On each page a color engraving of a peach, which was itself of breathtaking beauty, but even more luscious, underneath, in periodic Victorian sentences, a description of each peach. Three hundred peaches, each described so that it could not be mistaken for any other peach, the shades of its coloration, the texture of its skin, the nuances of its flavor, so that you would know *exactly* which peach it was. Swallow lingered over the peaches until he was called to dinner. As he was grudgingly putting the book away, he saw a children's picture book, called *Tabby's Gone*, by Abigail Rain. Though he knew how high on the list of a boy's crimes it ranked not to come to dinner when called, and at that a Thanksgiving dinner, Thanksgiving dinner produced by five country women whipped up to highest intensity, he could not help opening *Tabby's Gone*. Instantly he fell in love with Tabby, though he had gone no more than three pages in before his father's voice (oh no, it had escalated to that) called up the stairs —Don't make me come up there after you. The next year Thanksgiving was at home, the year after that at his grandmother's, and then Aunt Dorothy died.

None of the librarians he meets has ever heard of Tabby, or Abigail Rain. But almost all of them are nice, and sometimes they even invite him home.

Heberlein take-home exam

Due Tuesday 7:59 a.m. <u>Absolutely no late submissions accepted</u>.

Write a well-structured essay in standard English sentences supported by specific details from the text. Make up a topic or pick one from the suggestions below:

Consider one of the book's patterns of imagery and show how it contributes to the meaning of the novel.

Consider the narrators as fictional device. What do they have in common? What are their differences? How do the characteristics of the narrators support the objectives of the novel? Are the narrators consistent? Reliable? If not, what do the inconsistencies and unreliability add?

Consider the novel's attempts to formulate standards of morality. According to this text, what are the problems with trying to make ethical judgments of human behavior? What are the problems with not trying? Is a coherent set of standards developed? If so, what is it?

The author says in an interview that one goal in writing the book was 'to compose a highly documented picture of one moment in American history.' Is this book 'highly documented?' How wide a range of human lives is included? How detailed is their presentation? Does the book succeed or fail as social realism? How would the book be different if set in a different time?

Why the title? How would the novel be different if it were called, say *The Nation That Is Not*, *The Alchemist's Apprentice*, *1974*, *Seven Sisters*, *The Fire*, or *Swallow*?

Recall Leslie Fiedler's statement that 'images of flight, alienation, and abysmal fare possess our fiction.' No points for showing that Fiedler's statement applies to this book (too easy!), but is there a sense in which Fiedler's ideas illuminate this book? For example, does thinking about Huck help us understand Swallow?

Hint for use in future essays on American literature: You can *always* apply Turner. How is the American frontier, or the yearning for the American frontier that is no longer, the theme of this book?

Think! What else should you *always* be able to discuss in an American novel? How about *Puritanism*? Can you see the themes of America's founding in this novel? (William Bradford, perhaps? Jonathan Edwards?)

An example of the above: Whether or not it is true that 'all American literature from Nathaniel Hawthorne to Robert Hunter is about the devil,' can you apply that generalization to this novel?

How about transcendentalism? Is this American author the heir of Emerson and Thoreau? In what ways?

Pick one take on American lit we have studied in this course and apply that perspective to this book. For example, what would Matthiessen have said of it? Parrington? Leo Marx? Blackmur? Winters? The Fugitives? Bruce Franklin?

Show how the themes or techniques of this novel have been influenced by one of the other authors we have studied this semester. (Free hint: for extra freshness points, argue that this novel is *too* influenced by one of the other authors we have read this semester. For example, 'This is the work of a man who has spent far too long studying Nathaniel Hawthorne.' Or 'It is pleasing to consider what this novel might have been had its author never encountered Faulkner.'

Consider the negative space: What is *not* in this novel?

> *Hail Nothing Full of Nothing*
> *Nothing is with thee*
> Ernest Hemingway
> 'A Clean, Well-Lighted Place'

T.J. decided to go back to Denver the next day, and Swallow didn't want to go with him. He was disturbed by T.J.'s defection, T.J.'s abandonment, T.J.'s betrayal. He felt he had to rethink every conversation he'd ever had with T.J., the way you recontextualize your whole life when you join A.A. He didn't want to do that in T.J.'s Datsun on I-80, with T.J. in it with him.

So T.J. left west and Swallow stayed. Then he suddenly ached for home. He had to be in Colorado or he would die.

His first ride refused to talk and left him on I-90 in Wisconsin. He was there for three days, on a dead stretch of interstate near nothing. He waved, he danced, he made funny signs.

The second most important thing about being a man, Swallow knew, was deciding on your own way and then letting all else be only the story of that way. But the most important thing was not being stupid. Swallow crossed the grassed median and the backward-bounds lanes and stuck out his thumb. The first car stopped.

They let him off at the Newark Airport. He was riding six or seven feet behind his shoulders now, and above, looking down through smoked glass, aged, aching, lonesome, through knife-slit eyes, no feeling in his body, unsure how to interpret the buzzing of human voices.

You can always get out the way you got in. You just got to go past all the same places.

He called Marla in Larchmont. She said to come over. He hitched a ride into the city and took the train. He knew from the ache in his molars that he'd been clamping his teeth again.

At her house he slept. He heard her kids come and go downstairs. He didn't know how long he slept. They made love. One of them would wake the other in the night. Sometimes he'd find himself alone in the house, staring into her mirrors and saying, over and over, at a moderate tempo, 'I'm dying. You're dying. I'm dying.' One day he got the shakes, wrapped himself on the kitchen floor in carpets from the hall, arms clasped around his shoulders, rocking sideways back and forth.

She came home with the children and found him there. That night she told him he had to go. He asked for money. She said she'd buy him a ticket and asked him where. He said New Orleans. He didn't know why. Maybe because he felt in serious need of coffee.

Gray had been working for Kilroy for three weeks, without any definite arrangement, without any permanent plan, more worried more every day about his long overdue contract with Inca. He knew he sounded like Jelly Cornfish saying it, but finally he caught Kilroy at coffee, and said —Kilroy, we need to figure out what I'm doing here.

Kilroy didn't respond the way Gray usually responded when Jelly said something like that. He sighed and said —You are absolutely right. I just haven't been able to get on Bird's calendar.

—His calendar? Gray said, not understanding at all.

Kilroy didn't understand what Gray didn't understand, and then he did. This outsider knew nothing about the internals of the Fire.

—We can do pretty much whatever we want. So long as we can make a reasonable case later that it was necessary. One night I bought a freightliner. On my credit card! But if I hadn't done it, I wouldn't have been able to get the gear where it needed to be. There's a major tight-ass CFO, you'll probably meet him, Christopher, that wants to see a receipt for every half credit, but as long as you have the receipt, and as long as the people around you agree that what you did was necessary, well, it was just what was necessary. You never have to ask anybody permission to do anything.

Gray waited.

—*Except* people.

As if quoting a line everyone in the organization knew by heart, Kilroy said—All we are is people. So it's the one thing we do real slow. Takes a general meeting to bring a new person in.

—In? Gray repeated, sounding dumb even to himself.

—Well, yeah. I thought you knew. That's what I'm talking about. I like the feel you got for the guts of these things. I'd like to have you with us.

The meeting was only three days later. Like everything else about the Fire, it was extremely loose. You couldn't tell exactly when it started, and nobody seemed to be in charge. It was in the dining hall. Kilroy loaded up a huge plate of food and took Gray around the room introducing him to everybody, saying what a handy guy he was with projectors. There was some heated discussion of scheduling which repeatedly broke down into smaller caucuses, some complaints from the hospitality committee about relations with nearby local governments, and then new people. The first new person was a young woman in hospitality. There was no discussion of her at all. Then Gray. A guy from the business office complained about the growing size of the tech staff. —We're doing something wrong. We shouldn't need that many people to keep the gear going.

Bird, who had been sitting with a group of women near the food line, his back to the discussion as though he weren't listening at all, said quietly —It's tricky gear, and we use a lot of it.

And that was that. Gray realized he had been naïve about nobody being in charge of the meeting. Bird was in charge of everything that happened here. He just worked hard to make it look like he wasn't.

The point was brought home later when he sat in the business office, surrounded by forms, talking with Christopher, the chief financial officer, about salary.

Gray waved his hands. —It's not like I care about money. I'd pay *you* to work here. It's just that I'm leaving a huge financial mess back home. Unfinished contracts.

Contracts was obviously a word to conjure with in the business office. Christopher blanched as though a stink bomb had gone off on his desk. Kilroy, trying to save the situation, held up a hand. —If you were handling it all yourself, Gray, how much do you think it would take to get you clear of all your obligations? In cash paid today.

Gray wrinkled up his face. The first answer that came to mind was that no amount of money would be enough. He had made promises to Inca. He needed to deliver what he had promised. Those were *moral* obligations. Then he realized again he was being naïve again. Business was business. What would it cost Inca to start the project over, doubly late now?

—A hundred grand?

Christopher whistled. Kilroy's face clouded for the first time. Gray despaired. His chance to leave the worlds and follow the Fire through deep space, and to have it bog down over this.

—Wait, Kilroy said, this is *Inca* we're talking about? This is *Inca*?

Christopher smiled. —Oh. We ought to be able to handle *that*. You want to call them or should I?

Kilroy shook his head. —Bird needs to call.

Christopher agreed, and as Kilroy went off to find him, Christopher reminded Gray —We're Inca's biggest customer.

Kilroy came back with Swallow in tow.

—Who you work for at Inca? asked Bird.

—Taylor.

—Taylor *Parker?*

That was the first time Gray saw Swallow do a truly broad grin. —Give me a telephone.

> *To see beyond the landscape, beyond every shape*
> *and shadow and color, that was to see Nothing.*
> N. Scott Momaday
> *House Made of Dawn*

The geography began to lose coherence, the way anything does when you see too much of it. At the airport he tried to exchange the ticket for cash, but because she'd bought it with plastic he couldn't. He hung around the line until he found an individual to sell it to, half-price. He hung out at the airport for a day and a half, until he befriended a woman who ran a courier agency and got a job.

In the next month he flew to Rio and back, from Toronto to Miami, Miami to Boston to Mexico City, and back and forth to L.A. maybe ten times. He stayed with friends of the agency head's, wore a jacket and tie, ate heavily, and read every magazine he could find, as if *Newsweek* would show him the way back to regular people. On all the planes, on the hotel beds, in the hotel restaurants, he devoured them. They were impeaching Richard M. Nixon. None of it made any sense. What used to be in underground newspapers was now in *Newsweek*, and nowhere could he find the sort of thing that used to be in *Newsweek*. The whole world had stumbled off the deep end.

He was at a party one night, at the house of some friend of one of the friends of the agency head's, when Sarah called. —Dal, it's Sarah.

The guy in the leather coat was explaining his politics very loudly to the woman who was repeatedly slopping wine out of her glass, and someone kept dancing into the turntable, thundering the house. Toots and the Maytalls were on the turntable, loud, and every time whoever it was danced into the turntable, the needle bounced around like artillery fire.

—Hang on, I got to find some quiet.

The phone had a long cord. He carried it down the hall.

—I've got to see you. Where can I see you?

—Oaxaca. Hang on, I've got to find some quiet.

He opened a door, found a broom closet, shut himself in, squatting down.

—Okay, Oaxaca. Oaxaca when?

—Hang on just a second.

He bumped against a shelf, and vacuum cleaner nozzles bombarded him.
—Just a second, just a second.

A hose clattered, half caught itself on the coats, flopped against him from twenty directions at once. He waited till everything found where it wanted to fall to, holding the ironing board back against a wall, looking straight ahead at the lining of a navy blue coat.

—Go slow, Sarah. Where are you? Where am I?

—I'm in Clemmons. You're in Houston. The people in Macon gave me the number.

—Oh. I was leaving for Oaxaca tomorrow. I'm at a party.

—When can I meet you there?

—What's today?

—Saturday.

—Monday?

—Where, on the zócalo?

—Zócalo at high noon.

—You'll be there for sure?

—You're coming from North Carolina?

I would explain to you how to get there. Only there is no getting there. There is just being there. First you are here, and then you are there, and there was no getting involved. No muscles employed.

Swallow showed me. But there was nothing to show. He used no words. There were no external tools involved: no trance-inducing music, no incense, of course no drugs. He got me there the first time, but I'm embarrassed to say I don't recall how.

It's not as though . . . with something like, say, meditation. You can put in words things another person can do to learn how to meditate. You can't meditate for them, and just give them the results. They have to do it themselves. But you can give them instructions. You can say —I want you to be the watcher. I want you to sit right here and watch as carefully as you can what goes on in your mind. Sit at maximum alertness, asking yourself, 'I wonder what my next thought will be?' And then when the next thought comes, don't react to that thought, and don't follow it where it wants to lead you. Just ask yourself again, 'I wonder what my next thought will be?' I'll be back for you in a couple of days.

In fact, Swallow did exactly that for me. Took me on a day-long Jeep ride over Utah rocks, left me a lean-to, a five-gallon jug of water, and those instructions. I could do the same for you. But I don't know how I would show you how to see the . . . well, that other way of seeing.

What in my head I have come to call Nothing. Just because I needed some mental shorthand for it. For a long time I called it 'the other nation.' At the time, Americans were searching for somewhere else to be a citizen of. Backpackers in Europe sewed maple leaf flags to their backpacks. Our soldiers deserted to Sweden. I knew a fellow who ended up in Aberystwyth. Going as far into the twelfth century as he could get, unimpeded in his flight even by the case structure of Welsh. We were all looking for that other nation, the nation to which we truly belonged. So when I found this other place, or, well, it's not really a place, when I found this other way of seeing, well, it's not really seeing, anyway, when I found it, though it's not really an it, I called it first, for a long time, *my nation*. Then that seemed far too possessive, as though I were trying to receive credit for it, or put myself above it, as when a singer talks about '*my* band.' So then I called it *the other nation*. After I had been calling it that for years, I came across an A.E. Housman poem containing the lines,

> In the nation that is not
>
> Nothing stands that stood before.

And that nailed it for me. The other nation is not a nation. In fact, it is not anything. It is just not at all. It is the nation that is not. But it is not the nation itself that is of interest, nor its notness. It is what stands there which has always been there. That which has always been. To which Housman gives the name Nothing. So now I call it that.

I can't tell you how to get there, but I can tell you what it is like. First the things you see become two-dimensional. Say you're looking out the window at your neighborhood. Say you see vine maples in fall color, dancing bamboo, sunflowers, pumpkins, grass, squirrels, chickadees, crows, parked cars, peeling paint on Victorian houses, and complex shifting broken light across it all. The first thing that happens is that all that becomes as if, instead of looking at it, you are looking at a giant photorealist mural of it. You lose none of the detail, only the dimensionality. If anything, the lighting effects increase, but they're all on a completely flat plane. Then the dimensionality comes back and the opacity vanishes. You're seeing *through* everything. It is not as though you are seeing through to other objects on the other side. There is no other side. There is *Nothing* over there. But instead of the objects obscuring the Nothing, as they usually do, now you can see through the objects, and see the Nothing.

Finally, and this doesn't usually occur for me, maybe only like five percent of the time, finally something really strange happens to my vision, and I'm no longer seeing objects at all. I realize they are merely tags, vocabulary supplied by my mind, shorthand representations of a more complex phenomenon involving vibrational waves. My puny brain lacks the muscle to see the complex interaction of the waves, and so it populates my field of vision with objects. When the objects turn back into waves, I realize that they are not separate *figures* on a neutral *ground*, but that *everything* is all one active pattern of waves, all in motion together the way flames dance in a fire. At which point the *I* who is thinking these things disappears, because that I is also in the wave pattern, together with everything else.

And that's as far as I've ever been able to successfully describe it in words, because after that you would need a whole nother vocabulary, and syntax, and then a whole nother set of semantic motives for discourse.

The hard part isn't really getting there. It's getting back. And then it's living in this world, pretending to live in this world, with other people, while all your cells still remember that other nation which is not, while your whole being still aches for Nothing.

> *Some lovely glorious Nothing I did see.*
> John Donne
> 'Air and Angels'

He was there after breakfast that morning, and so, it turned out, was she. Aerovias Oaxaqueñas took them to a fishing village on the coast. They camped at a trailer park on the beach, swimming, playing in the surf, cooking crabs over an open fire, and, eventually, fumblingly, making love.

The first night, Swallow asked her —You wanted to talk?

—Yes, I want to talk. You got somewhere to be?

So they didn't talk, for the first week, except about the sun, the sea. Swallow's madness lifted slowly. He felt his breath come back into his body, felt his vision merging with his eyes, felt his heartbeat. There were long walks holding hands. They flowed into and out of the surf, they flowed into and out of sex. He felt sometimes he couldn't tell where his body ended. One day biting a thumb he wasn't sure whose.

Swallow lay face down on a shirt. He wondered where he had acquired the shirt. They were a mile south of town. He was naked, in tropical sun, salt on his skin. The Pacific broke just off the beach and ran the water at his toes. It made the sweetest music. Sarah woke up and he asked her. —How long has Blue been gone?

—The day I called you. Two weeks now.

He told her everything.

She said this —He thought I'd talk him out of it, and he was right. Blue wasn't stupid. He was set in his ways, but he wasn't stupid. I could look at him and say, 'Blue. Be a human being. It's the highest you can be. There isn't higher than that. Try to go for higher than that, you lose that, Blue.' You know that, Dal. That stuff's just reflections, like the dog sees in the water, leaning over with the bone in his mouth. Don't you go for the bone in the water, Dal, you got the bone in your mouth. Throw it away, what he gave you. Throw it away.

—I don't think I can do that, Sarah.

So she threw it away. The next morning it was gone and she was sitting awake beside him, watching him.

—I threw it in the ocean. A mile from here. Way out as far as I could wade.

—That was wrong.

—I could have talked Blue out of it, but you're not that smart. I did it for you, not for us. I figured you probably couldn't stand to be with me any more after I stole your magic.

—I don't think I can be with you any more, Sarah.

Only he could. They spent three days more together there. It reminded him of the week he'd spent with Cindy, in a tent on the Gore range, after they'd admitted to each other that they were strangers and ought to be better strangers. No matter how much love there is, it's such a struggle, the two of you straining to carry it, like straining to carry a couch up the stairs. And when you quit, when you throw the couch over the railing, the relief is so sweet, you sit down on the steps and play like little children.

She flew out on Aerovias Oaxaqueñas. He ate a meal of snapper in town, wrote a few postcards, washed out his clothes at the tourist park, made small talk with several gringos, walked barefoot up the rocky street over broken bottles and open sewers to the post office to mail the cards, caught a bit of body surfing, had dinner with a Mexican family, then found an oceanic biologist and her husband just packing their things into a Volkswagen van. They took him all the way to San Diego. He made it home in three days from there.

In New Mexico, near Raton Pass, he met an old woman on a white horse that could barely stand under its own weight. Her coat had once been a man's, and once not black. Her face was lined as heavily as the coat. They passed her, in the rancher's pickup, and then later she passed him standing by the ditch waiting for the next ride, passed him on her broken horse then stopped just a few yards away, dismounted, reached into the ditch, pulled out a clear quart bottle, and dropped it into one of the sacks on her horse.

—That's a no-deposit bottle, Swallow said.

Her face was strong. The lines were like the grain of cheap pine—deep and wide. Her jaw was squared off like the bucket of a backhoe. Her mouth was held closed, as if it never just hung open. Her lower lip was exceedingly full, and cracked like an old baseball mitt from the sun. Her eyes were set in deep, shadowed sockets.

—Would you like a drink of water? she asked.

It was out of a wetsack, warm, vaguely muddy.

Most people who traveled with the Fire turned all their home world concerns over to the business office. Gray did that. A nice woman with spiky purple hair said she would be his caseworker and gave him a number to reach her. Over a light lunch, she asked him to spell out his wants. —We can do whatever you want. We just have to know what you want.

Gray looked around. The break room where they were sitting had nothing permanent in it. The table on which their sandwiches sat was not a table but an end-piece from the standard packing crates the Fire used for shipping all their gear whenever they moved, which tended to be about seventeen times a year. The bed Gray slept on at night was made from an identical packing crate end-piece. When the Fire left this camp, which would be soon, everything would go in those cases. Where they had been there would be nothing left, only an empty space, and in some new empty space they would be taking end-pieces off packing crates. Permanently temporary and settled in homelessness. He smiled at the woman who wanted to know what to do with what he used to call his home.

—I guess what I want is not to have to even think about all that any more. I don't need a home world. If there's anything in the universe I possess, I guess what I'd like is to no longer possess it.

She smiled. —You're a quick study. It usually takes folks a few months to get over all that. Usually I keep paying their rents until they finally decide it's silly.

Gray arranged for Turk to go shut his house down, take whatever he wanted out of it, sell the rest. Old Cat was already at Turk's, and reportedly happier there. The one piece of business that could not be delegated was Jelly. He wrote her a long letter that took sixteen drafts, and then, being Jelly, she didn't just go away with a letter, she called him, and then she called him again, and about a dozen phone calls later, she came to visit, although the trip across space must have been a huge expense for her. The in-person goodbye was intensely painful and exhaustingly tearful, and it went on a long time. But then Jelly was gone.

Gray really did know a lot about projector design. And now, instead of being a contractor engaged to grind out a consumer-level hack, he was on the crew of the most elaborate projections ever put on anywhere. He was always being called to push the equipment farther than it ever had gone. So rather than finding it hard to make himself work, he found it hard to make himself stop working, to realize after many hours he was in danger of doing damage to the equipment if he did not take a break. He found a passion in him he had never known he had. After a life spent mostly in passive disengagement, guilt and boredom, he found something he cared very much about. He got to see the Fire every time it happened, and his own work helped light it.

He found himself waking up in the night with ideas for how to improve the projectors. Kilroy would come in in the morning to find that Gray had been there all night, had melted down a dozen of the units in the process of his research, but the one he had running at the moment was hot-rodded into states no projectors had ever before attained. Bird started stopping by almost daily to talk over ideas with him. Eventually Gray's designs worked well enough to be used live. And he had never felt such pride as floating in deep space during a particularly poignant effect, and knowing the effect would not have been possible without his work – never *had* been possible, had never been seen before, appeared in this arrangement only because he created it.

The Fire licensed Gray's designs back to Inca, and soon was receiving more in royalties than they had formerly been paying for the gear.

The studious concealment of Nothing
John Ruskin
Modern Painters III v 10

He had been at Joyce's for an hour when his mother called.

He'd hitched a ride up Boulder Canyon with the liquid-voiced director of the children's section of the Boulder Public Library. They had a good talk. He knocked on Joyce's green door.

—Oh. Hello. Did you come to get your things?

It was a thing he never learned, although they kept offering the class. You go away, and when you return, sometimes they have changed and sometimes they have not changed, and you never know whether they will change or not. Who would have thought Joyce?

—Joyce, I just hit Colorado this morning. I've been warped by the rain and chased by androids and I'm looking for a place to shower. I thought you'd like to see me. I'm sorry.

—You can eat here. I'll loan you change for the laundromat. We haven't got an extra place for you to sleep.

A woman in a pony jacket came out and put her arm around Joyce's waist. —So this is the one, huh?

—Yeah. I'd recognize it anywhere.

— Huh. Well take your boots off before you track across my floor.

Her name was also Joyce, he learned. The two Joyces talked to each other over dinner and let him sit silent. He volunteered to clean up. The other Joyce helped while his former Joyce read the *Daily Camera*, warmed to him a little, offered him a floor for the night.

He knew what to say. What to say was 'That's okay, I'd rather not stay where I'm in the way.' He said —If you wouldn't mind, for one night, gone before breakfast.

Then his mother called. The other Joyce answered, looked at the phone as if it were a turd, looked at Swallow as if he had just laid it, and handed it to him, saying, —Jesus, they weren't lying, it's for you, and it's a woman.

It was his mother. She didn't even know he'd been gone. She called to say Uncle Sam had died. That morning, at the doctor's office, of all places.

—He was in there for his check-up, and after he was finished and the doctor told him he was fine and to put his clothes on, he was a long spell coming out, so they went back in to check and there he was on the table.

—He just died? Just like that?

—Just like that, and Jacob right there in the waiting room not ten feet away.

He switched the phone to his left ear and sat down at the desk. It was his desk. There were his heat circles on it from cups of tea he'd drunk married to Cindy on South Logan Street. The edges were butt-charred. By the Luxo-Lamp a blob of black that was melted brush handle. His father had given him the desk, the desk his father's father-in-law gave him when he went into business, covered now with potted plants, orange peels, record albums, full of he didn't want to think what.

—He'd taken Sam to the doctor's, don't you see, and he was waiting there and they just made him wait, they didn't tell him a thing. Then when the nurse finally came out and told him to go back in, there Sam was with his chest cut open and blood on everything, where the doctor had tried to start his heart, don't you see.

The huge, fat, fleshy old man, loose lips and baggy pants, giant rocky knuckles, suspenders, flat carpenter's pencil in his t-shirt pocket, the hanging ears, red-lobed, his cavernous hacking cough and country laugh.

—Did he have a heart attack?

—They don't know. They're going to do an autopsy. And when Jacob called here I told him I'd have your father go break the news to Aunt Absolom, she works just across the street from the Capitol, you know, in the annex there, across Fourteenth, where they have the switchboards, but by the time Daddy could get there, just across the street, Aunt Vye had already called her and she was in hysterics.

—No.

—Yes. Vye's always been that way, don't you know. The minute Jacob called home to tell her, she just had to call Abbie, she just called up and said 'Abbie, Sam's dead,' just like that.

His mother was quiet for a minute and over the phone he could hear the dogs barking at something, King's growl, Butterball's manic yap.

—How is Dad taking it?

—It hasn't really hit him yet. You remember when John passed away how he was.

Knees crumpling before the coffin, five brothers, that high choking noise seeming to come from another room. For the two days before the funeral, it was like Memorial Day picnics, backyard eating off paper plates, competitive exchange of corny jokes, teasing the children. Then in front of the coffin, Sam's collapse and eerie sobbing, Uncle Sam with the wide back on which three or four children could ride. Uncle Sam unable to stand, four pallbearers holding him up. And his father.

—Is Peter flying in?

—I'm sure he is. Daddy called him early this afternoon. He'll have to see if he can get time off.

Swallow asked when the funeral would be, and if he was needed at home. They didn't know yet about the funeral, and no, they were doing okay, he should just stay and work on his studies.

—Are you sure, now?

—Yes. Uncle Sam wouldn't want you to interrupt your studies. You know how proud of you he was.

—Okay, Mom. Good night. You take care of yourself.

—Don't worry about me.

She called back in the morning, no one up yet, to say Aunt Abbie was having them all over for dinner that night.

—The folks at the home, don't you see, where Uncle Sam worked, wanted to have a dinner for her. She thought she'd feel better if she could have the brothers over. You don't have to come, of course. I'm sure Abbie would understand.

— Of course I'll come.

Title:

Every Man Must Build a Home

Structure:

A very short novel (less than 50,000 words) composed of: 1) a dual introduction; followed by 2) a body of straight narrative, about twenty takes of approximately one thousand words each, in a unity-of-time progression, in third person, from a limited point of view close to the protagonist; interspersed with 3) short narratives and expositions in a variety of voices from various points of view, offering parallax, side views, and metatext; opening into 4) a second main narrative thread; all stitched together by 5) epigrams in which the word *Nothing* can be misunderstood to create an alternate meaning.

Plot:

An American male, aged twenty-three, travels from Colorado to New York, North Carolina, and a small beach town in Mexico, then returns to his ancestral home when informed that his Uncle Sam has died. After a family dinner, he drives up a nearby mountain and decides not to kill himself.

Subplot:

A band of deep-space image artists confronts the exhaustion of the material universe.

Concerns:

1. If one accepts that 'home' is not and cannot be an objective place, that once anything has been a home, it can never be one again,

and that life as we know it is a continuous progression of creating and abandoning homes—

What variety of homes are created?

When, how, and why are homes abandoned?

What is the relationship between home-creation and the remainder of human activity and consciousness?

What sort of morality is required for the progression?

Is the progression constant, or is it accelerating? Is it *functional*? Can man's creative powers keep pace with his critical powers, or will he be forced to abandon homes he has yet to create?

What about other homes? When is a home not a home?

2. If the opposite of 'home' we call 'fire,' implying a perpetual simultaneous creation and destruction—

Is it possible to conduct a satisfactory life—or any life—in the fire? (c.f. Pater, 'to burn always with a hard, gem-like flame')

What is essentially human? In what ways is this essential humanity congruent with fire?

Can fire become a home?

3. If on a third axis from 'home' and 'fire' is 'Nothing,' (vide Sartre et al.)—

How does Nothing allow us better to see the *things* in which we conduct our human existence?

Conversely, how does knowing there is Nothing disable a human from living among things?

Is fire possible in Nothing? Can a home be built of Nothing?

Uses to which funds will be put:

1) The primary grant is requested for subsistence, to sustain the author while the manuscript is completed.

2) Should the supplemental amount be available, it will be used to retrace the protagonist's journey to verify geographical details.

> *Was startled when an answer really came.*
> *'Nothing.'*
>
> Robert Frost
> 'The Fear'

How finished the house looked. His father had been building it the whole time they lived there, one addition following another. It was never just a house, it was always a construction site. Now it wasn't. Now it was a finished house. And the finished house had a unity Swallow hadn't foreseen. His father had had a vision of how it would look when it was done. Swallow had never thought of it being done.

From the driveway he could see a crack in the family room. His father had built the original part of the house from cinder blocks, used cinderblocks from where they'd taken apart a storage shed down by the river. The northeast corner of the house was subsiding, and a crack had opened up.

His mother came out to kiss him. He took it on his lower neck, shook hands with his father. Everyone said it was good to see each other. They were drinking coffee at the kitchen table. He asked about his grandfather.

—He's down home.

—I'll pop down and see him.

He kicked a yellowed hunk of quartz down the dirt path. His grandfather was sitting on the wood steps of his back porch.

—Sam was up to the house three, four weeks ago, wasn't even hacking like he used to.

—How're your trees?

—Lost a couple pear trees last winter, and the apple up by your ma's. All the young elms.

—Those elms. They snap in the first good snow.

—Make good shade if you get them past grade school, though. Nothing like an elm for shade. You got time for a game of cribbage?

His grandfather had switched him from checkers to cards as soon as his hand was big enough to hold five of them. At nine he sat in regularly on the two-dollar poker games, his grandpa giving him two bucks and saying he could play as long as it lasted. It seemed like a long time until the day he had the two bucks at the game's end to pay back his grandpa, and seventeen cents to take home. Then one day he walked home with eight dollars and sixty-five cents. When he turned thirteen his grandpa stopped giving him the two bucks.

—Sure, I got time for a game of cribbage.

His grandfather got the metal board down off the mantle, pulled out of it the pegs he'd whittled for it, the cards. —Nickel a peg?

His grandfather took him for a dollar thirty-five the first game. He won twenty cents of it back the second.

—You learned a lot about pegging since you was in short pants.

—Comes a time it's easier to learn it than go on paying for not knowing.

Halfway through the third game, just as he was turning up third street, his grandfather six bits ahead, his mother called. They were getting ready to go, he should come on up. They finished the game and thanked each other.

—I wanted to ask you. You moved onto this place when you were thirty-six? Did you think you'd still be here fifty-six years later?

—I picked this place careful. I never had me a place of my own. I was all over this country. I rode this country since before I could walk. I looked at it all good. We're up here on the hill, where it don't flood. We get the sun. Over by Cecil's, he's in front of the canyon, where he gets all the wind. Yeah, I picked it. I figured to be here forever. No way to know they was going to build a nuclear waste dump just up the road.

Swallow had read his grandfather's correspondence school courses in carpentry. They were more historical and alien than the *Aeneid*, explaining how to make level lines with a plum bob and chalk line.

—Did you have a bubble level?

—I did for the porch there, not for the main house.

Swallow had been all over the house, since he was a baby. Down in the cellar, the stone masonry that was the foundation. He remembered the chapters on roof trusses. If he knew he was going to be marooned on a strange planet, that was the book he would want.

—How long it take you to build the house?

—Two years. We lived in a tent there by where the garage sits, we just had the girls then, George was born in the house, first month we were in it. August fourth.

—What kind of tent?

—Old army canvas. Big flap on one end with screen, so you could open the whole side up in summer.

In summer. He hadn't been imagining hard enough. —You were in it two winters.

—Just one. First one we were renting in town. Moved out here when it got warm. I'd never built a house before, I thought I'd be finished by fall. It was a good winter. We ate good all winter. We weren't paying rent, and I wasn't saving every nickel to buy a place. On payday, I'd get off the streetcar in Englewood, I'd walk into Rudy Schneider's and say, 'Rudy, cut me two pounds of your best.' You going to be staying long?

— I got to get back up home tonight. I'm driving a borrowed car.

His grandfather nodded.

—I'll have to come back down for the funeral. Maybe I can stay a couple days then.

Swallow lived in a stone hut deep in the woods. She was a servant girl. She came from peasant stock ('clumsy peasant stock,' her master so frequently reminded her). When she was very young, her mother died and her father bound her out as a servant to a sea captain's family in the port city of Spocketon. Later the captain fell on hard times, and her contract was sold to a necromancer.

The necromancer lived alone, far from town. He was exceedingly tall, with skin so pale his blue veins showed through, and hair white as milk. Very infrequently he entertained a visiting wizard, and Swallow prepared delicacies in accord with the necromancer's exceedingly detailed instructions, but most of the time, the necromancer spent his days and nights locked away alone in a tower a hundred yards from the house. Swallow had strict orders never to disturb him there. At noon and at dusk, she would carry a bowl of soup and a slab of hot bread, under a silver cover, out to the tower, where she left it on the step.

She scoured the floor and walls of the hut, washed clothes, tended a vegetable garden, and kept goats and chickens. But still she had long hours of each day to daydream, to remember the bright sails on the harbor at Spocketon, to imagine voyages to distant lands, herself a rover, or a fine lady.

The necromancer was not cruel. He never beat her, or took advantage of her the way other masters might. His demands were exact, but they were limited, and though he criticized the quality of her work and condemned her best efforts as hopeless, he seemed to expect no more, requested no improvements, and left her almost entirely to herself.

She would have had little to complain of, except for his familiars. He kept them in jugs—earthenware jugs, two-gallon jugs, stopped with cork and old rags—lined on a high maple shelf above the hearth. They were demons he had vanquished and captured. Sometimes he would take a bottle with him to the tower to help him in his work, but most would sit undisturbed on the shelf for months. Some rested quietly in their captivity, but others would howl. At night, on her straw pallet by the hearth, Swallow would wake from a frightening dream to hear Koutek rasping faint and high pitched, like a dry whisper.

A few times—for all his stern fastidiousness, the necromancer seemed somewhat careless in his work—a demon would come unbound, fly out of the bottle, and fill the cottage. Javik got out one spring and was loose for a day and a half, until the necromancer, finally distracted from his work by hunger and wondering why Swallow had brought him no soup, returned to bind Javik more tightly. Out of the bottle, Javik had manifested as a purple fog, keening, smelling of ore, deadly cold. He menaced and mocked her, but she stayed, as the wizard had taught her, on her pallet, inside a circle within a painted star. When Javik pressed too fearfully close, she lit a circle of candles around herself, closed her eyes, and sang songs of her peasant youth far away. Swallow fought bad dreams of Javik for weeks thereafter, but she never saw him again.

She never saw most of the jugs' occupants, though she knew many by smell. Dovig was something bad burning, animal flesh on fire. Skadhin was a sharp stench like the piss of some unimaginably ugly creature. Grov was like mold. Only Koutek had no odor at all.

She smelled them because the stoppers on the jugs leaked. She would often catch a whiff of unpleasantness and know that Afrok or Bij was seeping into the cottage's air. And, because she could not sit all day in her circle in the star, these seepages would sometimes get into her, and she could feel them at work inside.

Bij was a mischievous spirit, and when he was in her, she became clumsier than ever, dropping crockery, spoiling the butter, slopping dishwater all over herself. Skadhin was straightforwardly sadistic. When she had breathed too much Skadhin, she would stick herself with needles, burn herself badly on the fire. Afrok would arouse her, until she clutched her private parts, rubbing them to make the itching stop.

The worst was Koutek, who lurked where she could barely know it was him, got inside her own voice in her head, told her she was worthless, called her ugly names, replayed every clumsy mistake she had ever made, went back over every failure, and mocked her dreams as not only hopeless but also laughably shallow, pathetic creations of a stupid peasant girl who lacked even the imagination to make up better stories with which to console herself for her pitiful life. Koutek's damage was the deeper because she had such a hard time seeing it was him. She thought it was her own voice, telling herself what was only the truth.

Sometimes he would be in her for weeks before (the necromancer taking the bottle out to the tower, or adjusting the stoppers) she got a reprieve. And when he was gone, she still found it hard to believe it had been him all along. It seemed so real, so true. Without him, she felt light, she felt free, but, truth told, she felt guilty. As though without Koutek to point out her failings, she might be stuck in them forever. It was almost a relief when he came back, when she heard once more the familiar voice in her head spelling out for her just exactly in what incomparable ways she was so irredeemably stupid.

Barbed wire

Stories

Mobility and means of transportation

Trees

Money and economic transactions

The love of men for women

Children

The fact that Swallow's grandfather, in four separate occurrences, remembers his life in terms of barbed wire; that Diane's voice (a recurrent topic, remembered once as 'lazy, floating serenity') is linked twice to barbed wire—once with 'tension in it like tension in barbed wire when you're stretching it, hands sweating on the straining crowbar while grandfather with the hammer fumbles in the can of staples, clumsy in the thick gloves,' once rusting and coiled in great loops, 'like the barbed wire behind Grandmother's barn'; the central episode from the past when Swallow, trying to crash a party which had been over for hours, got into a fight with a barbed wire fence.

Grandfather's hair = old apple = the way he drinks his coffee = 'Did you think I'd forget you so soon?'

Old apple = Grandfather's well = burial.

Seventeenth Avenue in Denver, in the first days of the freak explosion there. That one weekend there, the girl after Diane, Blue before he went East.

Interchange with T.J. about fire and about timing.

Morrison, the old sheriff in his pink and green cowboy shirt. The Pillar of Fire Baptist church. Sunday traffic. The historical society marker in the bark-covered roadside park by Bear Creek. The teahouse where Diane worked one summer.

Morrison road. Peterson Turkey Farm. Peterson Field, where little league baseball was played. Uncle Sam's old house, behind the lawnmower repair shop. The inside of the lawnmower repair shop. Uncle Sam helping build Swallow's father's house. Mother with the shingler's hammer, father bargaining with the demolition contractor for used cinderblock. The great hole in the ground for the new part of the house, what the earth looked like, the layers of sand, clay, and gravel. Wild berries. The summer Swallow was a door-to-door salesman. The septic field in the pasture.

Nothing 'gainst Time's scythe can make defense.
　　　　William Shakespeare
　　　　　　Sonnet 12

The dinner was bad. Even the food was wrong, brought by the people up at the Home. No Aunt Vye's cold green beans with cheese, no Aunt Tillie's Jell-O with apples and raisins and whipped cream, no Uncle Jacob's noodles. All the people were the wrong age, and there were no children.

It was supposed to be a family gathering, but the family had always gathered and folded around the children. Big people sat in chairs around the edges of the room. The children had the center. Old people started talking by talking about the kids. The women got to talk baby talk. The men got to tell stories of their childhood on the Eastern Colorado homestead. Aaron hitching up the collie to the kindling wagon, the collie tearing through the barb wire fence with Jacob aboard. Jacob talking Swallow's father into wiring the outhouse seat with the coil from the truck, getting Aunt Bertha right across the wide expanse of Bertha's wide butt. The stories were real, the way books were, the way school was not. And then Uncle Sam, down on all fours, wide enough to seat three or four riders.

Swallow's cousins didn't have children. Hell, right now none of them even had a spouse, though all of them had at least one ex. None of them wanted to be horsie yet, they still wanted to ride. Swallow was the only one at the dinner. Sam and Abbie's son Stanley was said to be somewhere in Mexico. They'd thrown him out five years back, told him never to come home again and so far he hadn't. Swallow wondered if Stanley knew his father was dead.

He sat in the kitchen chair in the corner of the front room and ate his dinner off a paper plate on his lap and didn't have seconds, and after they ate, when they should have been all over the floor, they sat in the same chairs, and the women discussed small slights and the men watched a night college football game on independent TV, criticizing the announcers, inert in their chairs, old, mostly fat, breathing heavy.

There were just the four of them now, with John and now Sam gone. John had been the oldest, and then Sam had been the oldest, and now Swallow's father was the oldest, with his heart already half grafted from his hip, with his breathing like six Holly carbs when you've got the air filters off and looking straight down them.

Until he stopped trying not to think about his father and started trying not to think about his children. He hadn't thought about them in a long time. Even the dreams had gone, the waking visions of them purple-black and red in the bottom of the gleaming stainless steel sink, bubbling up again and always again again as a small, frightened nurse with very white hands kept pushing them down the grinding and churning and spitting and bumping disposal, bubbling up again always blue-black purple and red.

Diane, and her dull brown curls, stubby feet in clean white tennis shoes, and the hollow of her jaw, and then the shoulders. Swallow wanted to date, and Diane wanted to discuss the absurd. One day she came running up to him, literally running up the lime-green concrete high-school hall—they were just the color of Aunt Tillie's Jell-O, now that he thought of it—shivering, red-eyed, twisting her hands like rope, asking him to take her *away*, right *now*. She could not endure another thirty seconds. He didn't, of course.

Boy, it's useless to wish you were someone other than who you are, but if you were going to wish that sort of thing, don't you wish that just once you could have been there when Diane wanted, instead of suddenly waking to it with an ache years later?

Two other times, at night, driving the freeways, she asked him to leave with her. She had a friend in San Francisco who would take them in, Hashbury '67. I don't care what he told you about San Francisco. Did he tell you he met Janis Joplin? All about how he could have been the one to save her? He never got to the Summer of Love. Diane talked him into going, one Friday night when their parents thought they were at the movies. They were just driving the freeways in her Volkswagen, which is what they did whenever they did what she wanted to do. They were on Sixth Avenue, headed west, and she filled him up with the idea of it. They were already headed west, all they had to do was to just keep going. He could hear those words, in the melody of her voice, these years later.

—All we have to do is *just keep going*. Halfway across North Park, still in Colorado, Diane asleep in the passenger seat, he turned back. She didn't wake up until the city streetlights, and even then only gave him that same sad smile, the same way she always looked when he tried to tell her how much he loved her after they had sex in the car.

When she went to Kansas City for the abortion—it was illegal all over then, but her sister knew a man in Kansas City—Swallow wouldn't go with her, and the week she was gone was the week of SAT's. Swallow didn't sleep all week, knowing she would come home hemorrhaging and die, her insides falling out bloody onto her mother's pale carpets, and the doctor would know how she died, and he would tell her parents, and they would know. For a week, the shape of her face as she spilled herself dripping all over the carpet. But she came back Diane, and thereafter her parents wouldn't let her even stay after school for drama practice.

She finally gave him up as hopeless, stopped searching him out in the halls. Sometimes they ate lunch together in the court outside the cafeteria —against the rules, of course, Swallow looking over his shoulder for assistant principals. Diane talked easy and bizarre as ever, but she seemed to talk with even less hope that he would ever understand. He did catch on eventually, but by then they were thousands of miles apart at college. He wondered what she was into now that he still hadn't got to. He wondered what her baby would have been like.

After the football game Aunt Abbie wrapped up half a plate of cookies in waxed paper for Swallow to take back to Boulder. He'd driven Joyce's car over rather than riding with his parents so he could get away then. So he did, left them all there, Abbie weeping and whooping, the other women jockeying for position at her elbow, the men pretending to try not to look. He tripped on the way to the car over a three-foot-high dead tree Sam had tried to start there by the concrete driveway, in the new development.

He remembered all over again, as he tried to find the light switch in the strange car, how Cindy's had devastated him, when he finally heard about it from a friend. She never asked him, never even told him.

Diane Statt called here last night. I was gone, skiing with my daughter. Beautiful day, all manners of lights splashed across the peaks, first white, then yellow, then the reds of sunset, then the silver of a full moon. Snow on spruce. Gorgeous, gorgeous, gorgeous, and I had more fun skiing than I think I've ever had. The year at the gym helped with the thighs and the stamina both.

My wife answered the phone, and Diane left a message. He can call back or not. Sure enough, that's Diane Statt.

I called back.

Anyone who has ever gotten a phone call from Diane knows they are unlike most conversations. Sometimes it is like the first communication with a hostage taker. Or with the hostage of a hostage taker. Or with a race just discovered in the mountains of a distant island. Or with your sister with whom you haven't spoken in thirty years.

Diane and I haven't spoken in something like twenty.

She used to call all the time, when I lived on Pearl Street. Four in the morning, three in the afternoon. At the edge of despair. Or just because she had realized something, and wanted to tell someone. Those of us who were on her list compared notes.

Diane speaks very precisely. Unlike me, unlike most of my sloppy friends, she enunciates every syllable perfectly, and she puts her sentences together as if reading them out of the *Encyclopedia Britannica*. She speaks very carefully, as if following a line of secret stepping stones across a marsh, delivering thoughts you know she must have been up all night working out.

When I called her back tonight, the first thing she wanted to let me know what that she did not want to open up communications with me. We needed to be very clear about that, before anything else was said. This was not the recommencement of a friendship. Or anything like it.

—Two and a half years ago, you sent me a post card, when your novel was published. You added a handwritten note to the bottom of the printed postcard. And, this is funny, it is as though you had written it in disappearing ink. It finally just *faded away.*

(Did I say Diane emphasizes certain phrases when she speaks? Draws them out and leans on them. With a little laugh after. Well, not laugh, actually, not a chuckle, but a vocal production in the rough contours of a laugh, communicating acknowledgement of irony, perhaps, but no enjoyment.)

—The handwritten message said that you wanted me to read the book because, I think I'm quoting correctly here, 'believe it or not, I do value your opinion.' And I do know that, T.J. I am obviously someone that you valued a great deal. And yet, over the many years we knew each other, you found so many ways to treat me with contempt.

—Yes, I think about that. I feel remorse about that.

—Well, I think that's appropriate.

But that is not what she wanted to say. When you talk to Diane, it's really not worthwhile stepping off topic, even to tell her she's right.

—I was thinking that if you treated something, someone, you did so obviously value that way, it must be that you do that to yourself as well. There must be parts of yourself that you value that you abuse in the same way. This conflict must go on in your own mind. In your own heart.

—It is a source of great pain to me, I said. But she really wasn't very interested in hearing my acknowledgement.

—So the reason I called was that I thought it might be of some use to you to hear this perspective from someone outside yourself.

I said that it certainly was of value.

—Well, that's it, she said. Then she reiterated that she did not want to hear from me again.

—Surely a postcard every four or five years would be okay?

—That's just about right, she said. And laughed that laugh. I guess you'd call it a laugh. It's not about anything being funny, but it's doing the same sort of thing with your vocal chords that people do when they laugh.

When Gray had been with the Fire for about a hundred years, the dire things Jelly Cornfish had warned him of began to impinge on the Fire's ability to go on. The cost of power had gone up a thousand-fold in constant units since he joined. Power was now the single largest expense of the organization. There was no way ticket prices could be raised to the levels that would be required if the power bills kept doubling. And it was not just cost. There were times when power was not available at any price. Many systems had imposed severe rationing.

Gray, Swallow, and Christopher were talking about it one day.

—Well, Bird, said Christopher, I don't know how we're going to go on.

Swallow smiled, that smile that he always smiles. —We can't go on, we will go on.

—Well, I know that has always been true. When we got ripped off. When we went bankrupt. When travel was banned during the war. When Jeremy left. But this is different.

Swallow smiled that same smile. —It's always different.

Christopher must have been tired. He'd been carrying a heavy fear, and Swallow wasn't being fair to him in refusing to admit how much it weighed. —Damn it, Bird. What are you going to do when we've stripped the last sun, and there are *no more raw materials left in the universe?*

Swallow didn't smile that smile any more. He sat down. He poured himself a cup of tea. He poured one for Christopher. He poured one for Gray. —Yeah, we have a problem, he said.

They drank their tea in silence. One thing you could say about Bird, he knew the value of silence. Gray had once read an interview where Bird talked about it. —In every arrangement, there should be a moment of perfect silence. That's the key to the whole arrangement, for me. Everything else is there to support and frame that one perfect moment of silence.

—Okay, Swallow said after they finished a second cup of tea. We have a problem. Let's describe the problem. Blue? You're our design guy. Tell me the design problem.

Some years back, Swallow had taken to calling him Blue. Blue was someone Swallow had known a million years ago, and Gray reminded Swallow of Blue. Or, the way Swallow put it, 'I think you're him and you just don't remember.'

—We're a traveling band of artists, Gray proceeded slowly, who desire to continue presenting our works. Our works are creations shaped of phenomenal amounts of energy. The energy comes from fusing matter. We're running out of matter. There's a finite amount of matter in the universe, and you can plot on a graph the line approaching zero. There is not enough matter for us to continue on as we would like to do.

Swallow and Christopher nodded. There was more silence. There was more tea.

—So what we're looking for . . . Swallow prompted.

Gary was surprised. Then he was surprised that he was surprised. Although he thought he was the most creative designer in the universe, he was following Swallow for the same reason everybody else did. Swallow took you around the corner, when you hadn't even realized there was a corner to take you around. This one was such a simple corner. Gray had stated the problem. He hadn't talked about the design requirements, the search space.

—We're looking for a way to keep going, Gray temporized, realizing it was only a baby step toward the answer.

—We're looking for energy that hasn't been found before? Christopher attempted. But all three of them knew that wasn't it, so nobody even bothered proposing to look for matter that hadn't been found before.

—Here's what it is, said Swallow. We have used up the universe. So we need another universe.

Gray shook his head. —I don't think so. I think the current verdict from the cosmologists is that this is the only one. I'm pretty sure they're pretty sure about that these days.

Swallow smiled that smile of his. —Okay, so we *create* one.

Gray and Christopher looked at him, the way people so often did, all through his career, all through his life.

—Well, *this* one got created, didn't it?

> *I saw Nothing that I had not expected to see.*
> Roger Zelazny
> *Guns of Avalon*

Sam and Abbie had moved about two years before he died, from the tiny alfalfa farm up by Morrison into the new development that went up just east of the first rise of the hogback, where the old road used to curve around a series of lakes the size of stock ponds, where Swallow's grandfather had taken him perch fishing once and he had caught his first fish and his grandfather made him throw it back for size. It was hard to find his way out in the dark, streets all curving in on each other, lapping and circling and dead-ending, but one eventually led out, and he drove towards Golden, shocked by the amount of traffic.

Halfway to Golden he decided to drive up Clear Creek to the Peak-to-Peak Highway home rather than going up 93. Almost to Golden he decided to turn off first and drive up Lookout Mountain. He felt stupid for not having realized earlier he was going to turn off and drive up Lookout Mountain.

There was always a little cluster of houses at the foot of the mountain where you turn off Highway 6, but now there were new ones farther up with fresh sod still showing strip marks, and farther yet sidewalks where there would be houses but weren't yet. You come right out of that, though, up onto a face where the road is cut into the rock and there never will be houses, and it's that way all the way up until it rounds out near the top, and then they begin again.

Swallow listened to the motor pull and remembered driving the north face in a fog so thick Diane had to get out and walk beside the car, kneeling down now and then to look for the edge of the road. It was a wonderfully clear night. The stars and Denver twinkled madly. Joyce's Saab held the corners like a barrister holding his hat. He'd always climbed it before in old cars, usually Volkswagens. He tried a line through the long hairpin, blacking his lights first to make sure he owned it, but four cars headed down came on him all too quick thereafter, and he decided not to try a more vigorous climb. Maybe wait at the top till like four in the morning, come down and run up it once hard? How often do you get the chance? When will you be back?

Maybe run down it once hard and straight. God, Joyce's bathtub, how many months ago had it been? And that was like the first time he'd decided in, what, five six years? He used to decide every week? Did he really used to be serious, or was he just massaging erectile tissue of the brain?

He found now the lookout on the top, by the beer joint where they didn't ask for ID on week nights, by the tourist trap grave of a man who lived a lonely life out on the plains below, slaughtering away at the seemingly inexhaustible sixty million buffalo for their hides, leaving the tons of meat for the coyotes and insects and birds and sun, who became a national hero in his later, pathetic years when a pair of yellow journalists from Denver wanted a wild west show to tour with the circus they owned and found the old drunk looked as powerful as ever if you combed the snarls and small bugs out of his long white hair and put him in a new buckskin suit with Indian beadwork done by immigrant German women, and they made good money off him, they still make good money off his grave.

He looked out over the lights spread halfway to Kansas, nearly to Cheyenne. However ugly in daytime, the city was a wonder at night.

God, he could do it tonight. What was to stop him, the obligation to return Joyce's car?

How had he used to think of it, back then? His reasoning had been torturedly verbal, legalistically syllogistic. It was like trying to remember verses of songs you hadn't sung since you were a kid.

Here: if you've made a morality that lets you not have to decide all the time, but only as rarely as you can make it work, there are two things you have to teach yourself to do. One thing is to teach yourself not to decide all the time. That's hard at first, but not after a while.

He knew every turn. He'd imagine a sharp cock of the right wrist on the wheel, just this much, a motion that wouldn't even turn a doorknob, *just this much*. God, he remembered sitting in science class looking at his right wrist, thinking, just this much, just this much. You couldn't think of it all the time, it didn't leave any room to think of anything else. So he made the morality that said whatever he decided on Sunday night was good for the rest of the week, and he didn't have to think about it again until the next Sunday. It was hard at first, but eventually it was like having no morality at all.

Then came the second thing you had to teach yourself to do, and that thing gets harder instead of easier, and that is to make the times when you *do* decide meaningful decisions, so that you *will* have a morality. It is hard and it just gets harder, until it is so easy not to decide at all, ever, just to allow your trained ability not to think about it to carry you along.

And is that what had happened? Had it just become automatic, and now he never decided any more? Could he remember how to decide? Could he decide once tonight, once for maybe the next two years? Would it be a real decision? Were they then?

He remembered the process then, like remembering how to disassemble a Volkswagen fuel pump. Step outside. Step outside. Find everything you're inside, one at a time, and step outside.

Step outside everything, and don't look back at it. See if you can make one new thing.

He realized at some point that he was very cold, and then he realized it was gray where it used to be black. He realized that he knew what he was going to do. He was going to try to find Diane.

> *The listener, who listens in the snow*
> *And, Nothing himself, beholds*
> *Nothing that is not there and the Nothing that is.*
> Wallace Stevens
> 'The Snow Man'

I ran across him two years later in the Tulsa freight yards. They've made Tulsa into a seaport, dug a ditch down to the Arkansas, which runs to the Mississippi. Then the Gulf. I figured I could find something going west. I was walking into the yards when he came up beside me.

—Shouldn't go in that way. Guard in that shack there. Where you going?

—Thanks, I guess. Oregon.

— Mind if I go with you? Here, let me show you how.

I followed him out of the yards, through the warehouses to a bar. He went straight to the phone, dug out the yellow pages, dialed, talking all the time how Tulsa was such a bitch, all tank cars for oil.

—Hi, my name's Mason, DX By-Products, I got a trailer to piggy to Portland, what you got goes that way? Sure. Wouldn't have their number there?

Dialed again.

—Should have thought of Burlington right off.

Same story.

—Too late to load for that now? When's the next one? Certainly, I'll do that.

To me —We're in luck, kid. 6656 for Seattle this very afternoon. Really ought to call a week ahead.

—Pretty good trick.

—Pays to do things right. Could I hit you up for food?

Greasy hamburgers. We walked to a liquor store, where I bought some bourbon and he picked up some empty pop bottles with screw-on lids, and filled them with water. He had me buy a bag of oranges. —We'll be glad we have these.

We climbed a viaduct to look through the jumble for our train.

—That's ours there. Look at it shine. The Burlington is the only line in America has painted its cars in the last twenty years, when they merged with Great Northern and NoPac.

A long train, four engines. Halfway back we found a good car, open, empty box, shredded packing paper at one end. We fixed ourselves a spot, settled in, and before we even left the yard he started talking. He kept at it, pretty steady, easy and slow, all the way to Seattle. It never seemed like he was talking hard, until you added up all he'd said, just like it didn't seem like I was drinking hard, until I went to get a taste and it's empty and it's still the first night, moon still low.

We talked mostly music to begin with. When we got to Judy Roderick, Candy Givens, Katy Moffatt, it was obvious we were both from Colorado, and we got to talking about the land.

—You go back much?

—Never. Miss it all the time, though.

—Why don't you go back?

—What I miss isn't there any more.

He threw my empty bourbon bottle out the open door. I watched the square bottle with its flat, round neck, its fine old label, paper seal announcing government approval, sail a one-and-a-half gainer out the door. I listened for clink or pop, but couldn't hear it over the pounding of wheels on rail.

—It's like a girl you can't sleep at night for seeing, maybe just one resonance that crept out of her voice one time when you weren't looking, one time maybe you almost had together, or one thing you think you maybe saw in her eyes that would be the only thing you've ever seen that would have made a difference, and you're lying there not sleeping until all the black seeps away and the things come back again. Only when you look her up when you're wired up on what you think you remember you find out things you forgot or never knew or what happened after what you knew which makes what you knew not real any more, nobody out there but this stranger who lives inside something which looks vaguely like what you remembered also lived inside of, and you could do just as good looking down garbage disposals and underneath cars as beating around there where the latitude is the same, what's living there now is just like all the stuff what you remembered was important because it was different from, the sounds that come out of it no voice only noise like everything else is making, no one could ever see anything through those eyes ever at all, and whatever runs the body so obviously bored and can't figure out what you're hanging around for, obnoxious and irrelevant, when she's in a hurry to get ready for her swinging date with a junior advertising executive, from the creative side of the business, of course.

I was choking on the dust. It was caking in my throat like the time Regina and I tried to camp in Nevada. I was thinking how there were things you could do with your logic, and how there were things you couldn't equate, couldn't weigh, thought about it in the silence his voice left. Colorado such an open, such an easy hurt, we may as well talk it with that.

—But nothing you ever see or don't see can keep you from going through all the remembering worse the next night.

—And the remembering seems so real, just that there's nothing for it to be real about is so undebatable, a man could get ripped into strips of bacon just slicing on the edges of it. You think we're going north? Burlington runs stuff through Denver. We could be in Colorado now.

He looked out at the dark.

—It's kind of nice not knowing.

—Yeah, but I remember when it was nice to know.

He stood and stretched.

—Last time I was in Colorado I worked as an arsonist.

He methodically stretched, stretching hamstrings, stretching quads, stretching deltoids while he talked.

—I worked for a construction union. I burned condos down. That's what they built the most, cause they go up so cheap. Course the houses were just the same, only instead of a wall in common they'd leave a foot to look at each other across. I specialized in what they called townhouse developments, they were so damned easy to burn. Maybe three, maybe . . .

He stopped in mid-sentence and I didn't interrupt. A hundred miles went by. I wondered how far away was dawn. I wondered if maybe when it started to get light we might sleep.

—Maybe four times in my life I did something I enjoyed. Feel my whole body in, use my wits, get excited, laugh. Just about the best I ever got paid, that counts, too. How much of the sprawl out in Jefferson County you see?

—Green Mountain. Columbine. Arvada heading for Broomfield.

—When I hired on they were heading up Mount Vernon Canyon. It looked like they planned to roll right over the Rockies.

Armies. Always they acted like armies.

—My grandfather once told me, looking out across the city from back by the feed bunks, that he used to be able to ride from Cheyenne to La Junta without having to cut one fence. But even after they trashed the plains, there were still the mountains. No matter how many squat cities they splashed on the plains, the mountains. You lived asphalt lives, but look up out of asphalt, there they'd be. All rippled. Singing an old song. You could go up into them, smell the soil, the soil which was just about half pine, pine bark, pine needles, and pine wood, you could breathe. Who could, however much they needed the money, who could, how could you drop a blade on Lookout Mountain?

L.A.Heberlein

You could if you were part of an army.

—And the marks coming in thought it was just great, after New Jersey, thought it was beautiful, they'd never seen it hard and empty, never seen the way it flowed on down, no eight-lanes up the canyons, only rapid crooked creeks, narrow beds out of that black dirt, little mica flecks, and at night with nothing moving and the huge black sky, blacker mountains up all around you, smell of that air, and the stars.

He didn't talk for a long time and I didn't either, lying very still in the packing paper, feeling the sound of the steel vibrate through layers of body, powerful heartbeat pounding from the outside in.

—Going flat out. In from L.A., doing twenty acres a day, they couldn't bother with details like watertight roofs, walls would crack before people got their stuff in, they built on top of coal mines, on plutonium from Rocky Flats. Floors buckling, plastic gas pipes exploding underground. I remember one outfit, out of Texas, I think they were, building up around Thornton, lost all the houses before they could sell them. One good wind, they all blew down.

—I remember that. Killed a couple finish carpenters.

—Didn't slow them down, though. Took off all directions. Out to Douglas County, east almost to Limon, up twenty-five. But especially west. That's what they sold in New Jersey, come to Colorado, live in the mountains. Even if they had to scrape all the trees off to make room for houses and gouge out the canyons for highways. Everyone was in on it, construction paid so hot, hipnoids swinging hammers, you could imagine them at home with folk guitars, then get up the next morning and kill another twenty acres. Yeah, well that's what the unions didn't like. Obviously they didn't mind the Cats up Turkey Creek. What pissed them off was all those skinners who weren't paying dues. All the organized outfits couldn't keep up with the boom, how you going to organize out-of-state congloms that blow in, cover a hill, then blast on out to Idaho the next week? Not to mention everybody's bro in Denver had an operation, using high school kids and borrowed money, filling in the irregular-shaped patches the big boys didn't bother with. Madcap building boom, everybody's shuffling dollars around, everybody gets to hold it for a while except the unions, twenty years of organizing, couldn't even get a piece. So they hired a guy to advertise the benefits of union protection. Just so happened I was the guy they hired.

While he told me how it got around to just so happening that way the train was entering a city. Every few minutes the diesel horn sounded three times. It didn't Doppler like a sob and fade away into distance like a train does when you're sitting still on the unmoving earth, listening to it pushing away. We were on it, riding it out. It held the same steady tone and intensity, a hard, solid crying out, not wistful and not ghostly – absolute, unremitting, immediate. Lights whipped and filtered through and across the boxcar, crossing reds, auto headlight whites.

—I enjoyed it a lot. I said that. Seeing a row of condos crumple, coals shooting maybe a hundred feet in the air. And getting paid for it. Paid for it, no less. I told them townhouses, that was my idea. See, all the inside walls are just curtain dividers, catch them when they're just about finished, it's one big air scoop, great big Japanese lantern, they do all the work for you, suck it on through. And the suction whips it up, and the load-bearing walls always buckle just when the roof has caught, so it's all uniform like a marshmallow all just tan, then the walls fall away and the huge burning roof comes whamming down like a hammer on a horseshoe. Like deep-rock dynamite in a narrow box canyon. All they can do is come pour water on the ashes. It steams and pops and you can watch the colors of fire refracted in steam and reflected in water.

—That's if they even have a fire department, right?

—Yeah, I forget you were there too, right, how they'd move in and find they didn't have water, or mail, or a grocery store, can't get a phone for seven months, the schools are in army barracks, no parks, no police, and the Lord better be watching if you smoke in bed. But even if a team of professionals were stationed all around the perimeter, those things were bombs. God, what you learn about how government works. I mean, all day long there were inspectors climbing all through them writing up tickets if the plastic pipes were four inches apart instead of five, but you'd look at the walls in a light breeze, or you'd see what a match would do. Ten minutes, tops. If I were chief I'd ignore it and pour all I got on the neighbors, cause when the roof comes down we're gonna splatter cinders for a hundred yards, and oh look what we got next door, it's one just like it. One night I had seventy acres on fire, sloping to a lake.

—Out by Jewell? Those two little lakes north of there?

—Yeah. They built on up west from that. Rebuilt it later. But I cleared it once for them. Better than the Ringling Brothers. Started up on the hill, rolling right down to the water, all the red and black in the water, buildings falling every two minutes, air full of noise and smoke and choppers, searchlights and explosions and water and sirens, great smoke, and chunks of trusses sailing into the lake.

We'd left the city. No more streetlight hollows in the darkness, neon bars and old motels, clanging red crossings. Nothing outside the car, black spilling in the door, unbroken, very black nothing, filled with unbroken rhythm.

—That was the last big easy one. After that they put up concertina, got these ugly Dobermans inside and armed cops outside. Sometimes inside, locked in their cars, scared kids in an old Chev, spotlights on top, circling the skeletons, one gripping the ten-gauge, dogs on the hood.

—That about when you quit?

—No, that's when it started to get to be fun. Gasoline and soap flakes is one thing, but it isn't very romantic. Now I got to try out some technology.

—Wasn't it just a couple days, wasn't there just a right time, you had to hit it just right? So didn't the security, wasn't it like they knew?

—Yeah. The insurance underwriters got awful touchy, and, well you know how it is with any repeated public crime, the newspapers scream and they put on a task force, and by the end there were more folks guarding at night than hammering in daylight. So you can't saunter in with your refilled cider bottles. Can't get in at all. Have to work from outside. Adds a whole new dimension. First thing I got into was a big fiberglass crossbow. You could lob a plastic sack of jelly right in there. I had spiffy little igniters I wired together myself. Or you turn on the gas main. They got two-inch open pipes in there. That's how I killed the guard. I quit after that. You see that in the papers? Just a stiff, from a small town in California. Wife and two kids. I didn't want to kill anyone's dad.

He stood up as though he were finished, leaned against the door.

—Smells like a river out there, he said, but I didn't figure out until later that that was what he said. I was in a reverie, embryonic, rocking in my new steel mom with her big steel heart.

I was on my own by then, underground. I only worked a year. I guess the unions got what they wanted, or got leaned on by somebody bigger, because I got a call to come see them at a motel on Colfax and when I got down there they gave me a big suitcase of bonus and said my services were no longer required. I figured I could live a year or two and work as a volunteer. They were way ahead of me. This one guy, a big guy, not the one who usually paid me off, he said to me, 'Now we don't want no more, now.' And I must have looked funny, cause he said, 'Next time a townhouse smokes, the arson squad might get an anonymous call from some concerned citizen.' So I told him straight out, 'I tell the D.A. a third of what I know and immunity smiles all over me for the next third.' And he stops smiling and says, 'You do what you want. You think it's cheap to buy a fire you ought to see how cheap a punk dies.' So I went underground, and I was going to work on. But the very next one was the night I killed that man. I was dead meat from the union mob, I was wanted for homicide. I decided it was time to find somewhere else I could love. Jesus, though, you ever seen, like you ever seen cloud cover along the front range with an afternoon sun behind it, poking through holes, and maybe one of those holes is straight down El Dorado Canyon, so it's like Griffith backlighting Gish, one big tube of yellow coming straight down El Dorado at you? I wonder what they did with El Dorado Canyon. You ever go up there just a week before spring?

I pushed and I squirmed to birth myself of out my balloon. I heard his questions, I had answers, but I couldn't talk. It was like waking from a bad dream into a burning apartment, trying to make limbs move but you can't find the connections. He leaned his body back against the door and tilted his head. There weren't even stars in the sky.

—And unless I'm there now I've never been back.

The train was coming around a long, tight curve, and its headlight was the first light I'd seen since the city, coming almost back in on us across a bend in a low, flat river. It gave him a silhouette, a skinny little kid, with a funny, loose way of standing.

—So what do you do now?

He looked around at me, head crooked back over a bracing shoulder, and smiled, outlined in the train's faint headlight reflecting off the river.

—I don't know. What does anybody do?

L.A. Heberlein has authored *Earthquake Babies, Sixteen Reasons Why I Killed Richard M. Nixon*, and the *Rough Guide to Internet Radio*. He edits the online literary journal *Square Lake* (www.squarelake.com) and distributes his personal journal to an email mailing list whose home is at www.heberlein.net. Born and raised on the Front Range of Colorado, where his great grandfather arrived on foot in the 1850's, Heberlein now lives in Seattle with his wife, the painter Gillian Theobald, and his daughter Elaine. He has worked as a college English teacher and a software entrepreneur. His previous storynovel, *Sixteen Reasons Why I Killed Richard M. Nixon*, is available from Livingston Press.